Green Eyes and Grandmas – How to Manage Year 6

By

Martin Clayton

Published by New Generation Publishing in 2019

Copyright © Martin Clayton 2019

First Edition

ISBN: 978-1-78955-535-6

www.newgeneration-publishing.com

New Generation Publishing

Dedication

To my incredible wife, Ali, and my wonderful children – Cal, Rob, Paddy and Billie-Rose – thank you for your love and support; I couldn't do this without you!

And to every child that I have ever taught – you probably aren't aware of this, but you are teaching me too! Thank you for the inspiration.

ONE

The single funniest thing that I've ever, EVER seen was on a football pitch at the local high school.

There was this girl (there's ALWAYS a girl, right?)... anyway, she was called Gemma Cook and she had long blond hair and blue eyes – more about her in a bit.

So, Gemma had a freekick and girls from Horley Juniors were lined up in a bit of a wall in front of her.

If you aren't sure what a wall is, then you're not alone – I've never been taught the tactics of a wall, so I'm sure the girls of Horley Juniors were relying on what they'd seen on TV during the World Cup.

Gemma was about 20 yards from goal – I'm making this bit up a bit – and, to be honest, I'm not sure what 20 yards looks like, but it seems like something a commentator might say... anyway, she began her run up and it was clear that she was about to aim straight for goal.

I'm going to stop here for dramatic effect (like I was taught by my Year 5 teacher, Mrs Barker) and also to introduce myself.

My name is Oscar Delta. My middle name is Charles and, yes, I'm named after the phonetic alphabet. This isn't relevant, except to say that my Dad (Mr Delta) once, before I was born, thought it was very amusing during a summer holiday in a pub, called (I think) the Black Swan – after he'd had a few drinks – to call me Oscar Charlie Delta, which, if you know your phonetic alphabet, is the acronym OCD. This provoked hilarious laughter apparently, but Mum must have decided it was a good idea and it did teach me, at an early age, what the phonetic alphabet was.

Anyway – I've realised I say 'anyway' a lot – mental note: STOP – at this stage, this was not only the funniest, but also the greatest time of my life to that moment.

I was sat, in the sunshine, with my best mate, Stevie Sykes, watching my girlfriend (she really was) play football. Year 5 was finishing in two days and the summer holidays were ahead of me. We had a family holiday booked to Florida (FLORIDA, in the U.S.A!) and my report had been an overwhelming success in our home, resulting in my dad calling me 'Hero' every time he passed me and doing that fist bump thing that people always seem awkward doing. I had actually begun to consider myself a hero.

Looking back at this all now, I can see that I should have expected the whole house of cards to topple in.

So… back to Gemma, with the golden hair – did I say golden before? I probably said blond, but thinking about it all now, it was more golden. You can actually see it, if you try, with the sun reflecting off it.

Sorry, I'm getting all maudlin – that's what my Auntie Julia says! It fits perfectly here. Suffice to say, Gemma was 'a catch', she was smart, beautiful and she liked football… what more could a ten-year-old boy be looking for?

When she kicked the ball, she did so with all her strength. The ball flew, like it was shot out of a cannon, straight at the wall of girls, who had no time to react, even if they did know what was coming.

There was this girl on the left side of the wall – I don't remember what she looked like, she's a bit-part player in this scene and her role was about to end – anyway (there I go again), she took the weight of Gemma's shot full on in the face. It was like one of those diagrams on the TV news when there's an eclipse and it shows coverage. In this case it was a total eclipse as one minute there was girl, then ball, then fresh air.

The girl dropped to the ground like she'd been shot.

2

At this point, we all (those of us watching: Stevie, me, some slightly interested teachers and some Year 10s, who were supposed to be in charge in a 'support' role) took an involuntary breath at the same time, which – if you think about it – probably altered the air pressure at Horley High for a nano-second. I'm guessing that we were all torn between wondering if the girl was ok and whether we were allowed to laugh. I mean, she did just disappear – as if she was a balloon and someone popped her!

The incredible thing was, whilst time seemed to stop momentarily and there appeared to be no sound, as if someone had pressed the mute button on the TV, like my mum always makes us do during adverts, there was one thing that was still moving.

Well, two actually.

The ball, which had eclipsed the Horley girl's face, was now rolling in the exact opposite direction, straight back to Gemma.

And Gemma, who seemed unfazed by the fact that she may have burst an actual live girl, was running forward to meet it.

I should point out, that – at this stage – we were all still on mute, but also on pause, whilst our brains were fighting to keep up.

Gemma, like a soldier in a battle zone, was operating in a sort of slowed down time, seeing everything, like that bloke in *The Matrix* (which is a film from twenty years ago that my dad says was a 'game-changer'); he's still moving at normal speed, while everything around is in slow motion, so he can anticipate and act before anyone else has chance.

Again, Gemma's contact was perfect and… again, the ball was like a bullet being shot out of a gun straight towards the Horley Juniors' goal.

And goalkeeper.

I do remember what she looked like, because I'd seen her before. In fact, she was the daughter of my mum's friend, Louise. She was called Megan and she'd always seemed quite nice, so it was a shame that she was the next balloon to get popped.

Once again, the ball hit her full in the face – the second eclipse we'd seen that afternoon.

And, once again, the result was fresh air where there had previously been a head.

AND, once again, there was a collective intake of breath from all watching, but this time I remember noticing that this included the girls on the actual football pitch, who were all stood open-mouthed, while two bodies lay on the turf.

AND, ONCE AGAIN, the ball was bouncing, then rolling... back towards the golden-haired Gemma, who (I'm not going to say 'once again' once again) was already ahead of the action and rushing to meet the ball.

Now it would be easy to say that we all expected this ball to be met by the same ferocity, driving it into the now-open goal, but, being honest (as I mostly am), we didn't... because we were still thirty seconds behind Gemma-time and trying furiously to catch up.

But that's exactly what happened.

And, once the ball was rolling around in the back of the net, some great celestial being released the pause and mute buttons and we all – collectively – began to cheer, laugh, grab each other and ask pointless, rhetorical questions like, "Did you see that?"

It was one of those moments that you try to tell to people later, but it never comes out the way that you want it to and never quite seems as momentously funny and incredible as it really was.

You really DID have to be there.

And so, I went home, still laughing to myself, with that warm, light-headed feeling when everything is brilliant and your place in the world around you is just perfect – like the feeling when you wake up in a warm bed on a Saturday morning and you know you don't HAVE to get up for any reason other than you actually want to.

ANYWAY… that's when the house of cards toppled in and the funniest, greatest time in my life to that point, gave way to the single saddest, worst time in my life…
   TO THAT POINT.

TWO

I mentioned that my report had been very well received at home and that my dad had kept calling me 'hero'.

Well it seemed that this was what educated (or old) people call a 'double-edged sword' – this is a particularly well-placed metaphor (I'm always thinking that Mrs Barker is marking my work).

You see, whilst one 'edge' was clearing a path for the hero, returning from battle to claim the spoils (metaphors EVERYWHERE here folks), the other 'edge' was simultaneously – that's a synonym for 'at the same time' – slicing through my perfect summer and the hopes and dreams of an ecstatically happy, ten-year-old boy.

How's that for irony?

So MANY writing points in this chapter already!

I think I need to move on.

THREE

I clearly remember closing the back door, calling out, "I'm home!" to the house, or anyone who was listening, and kicking off my Vans. I particularly remember the last part, because I felt quite happy with myself in that I was adhering to 'house rules' and I often forgot that part, only to get told off 2-3 minutes later, when I was spotted by a vigilant parent (parents are ALWAYS vigilant, when it comes to footwear indoors).

I remember that the kitchen was empty and there was a distinct lack of the smell of food – which, at this time in the evening, was odd.

Then, I recall the sound of the TV being lowered from the living room and my dad's voice calling out, happily, "We're in here, Hero!"

All good so far... if a little confusing and not normal operating procedure for mid-week.

I stuck my head around the living room door cautiously, not quite sure what was going on, but having the distinct feeling – like an inbuilt radar warning – that something was wrong.

Mum and Dad were sat on the sofa together, looking really happy – smiling broadly, in fact – and it was obvious that they'd been waiting for me to get home. I felt like asking them outright what was going on, but something held me back, maybe I knew that whatever they were going to say, I wasn't going to like it?

So... I just stood there, head poking around the door, looking at them both, beaming back at me from the sofa.

Finally, Mum broke the silence, "Aren't you going to come in, love?"

"Um, yes," I managed, as I eased the rest of my body into the room. But still, I stood, in the doorway, feeling like I needed to be ready to escape.

"How was the footy, son?" asked Dad, with the same grin on his face. What WAS going on?

"It was, um – yeah, it was great actually. Very funny, in fact."

"Good, good," said Mum. "You'll have to tell us both about it."

"O…K."

There was still a very large elephant in the room. Like a huge air pocket, which was poking into my tummy and making me feel really uncomfortable.

Pretty soon, either it, or me, was going to give.

"We thought we might go out for tea," said Dad. "To Aldo's. What do you think about that? To celebrate?"

Wow… Aldo's… we hardly ever did things like that.

The air pocket momentarily eased. Maybe my report was still greasing the wheels? I breathed out.

"That sounds great! What are we celebrating?"

Mum and Dad looked at each other briefly, the pocket expanded again and my tummy made an odd noise.

"You moving schools to Netherlea!" said Dad, with a look of extreme pride and happiness on his face.

The air pocket exploded and I was flooded with negative energy, my face clearly displaying everything I was feeling, as life – as I had previously known it – was destroyed.

FOUR

My mum is a cuddly mum – I'm not referring to her shape, which I couldn't really describe, because… well, to be honest I don't feel right doing it, but she has always been, shall we say, 'ready' with the cuddles.

I only realised this when I went to Matt Sanderson's 8th birthday party and saw how him and his mum never even touched. She brought out the cake and put it on the table, without evening looking at him. We all sang, Matt blew out the candles and she clapped and left us to get on with it. It felt odd.

I know that, when I got home, the first thing I did was hug my mum.

Mum always tells me that she loves me, all the time.

Again, about the same time as the Matt Sanderson incident, I realised that not all parents do this. I began to understand that I was lucky, that I have an affectionate mum.

Dad is affectionate too, but in his own way, in a manly way. He hugs me, but not all the time, preferring an odd fist-bump, or a high five.

I could see, straight away, in their faces, that Dad had talked Mum into this. Her face fell and she looked in Dad's direction. He avoided her gaze and looked out the living room window.

Suffice to say, we didn't eat at Aldo's that night.

FIVE

The next few weeks were torture.

To begin with, I was really upset. I made excuses to not be in the house and when I was, I spent as much time as possible in my room.

Don't get me wrong: I tried to reason with them. I begged them, I argued with them, I even cried, but it was no use. Clearly, the transfer was complete with the local council.

I even heard Mum on the phone one day, after a particularly upsetting family meal with my gran and granddad Delta, speaking to someone about the possibility of moving back. I got excited for a moment, listening from the upstairs landing, but then I heard her telling the person at the other end, "Thanks for trying," and she went back in the kitchen, where she announced to my gran and granddad that my place had already been filled.

Great!

Stevie acted like it was no big thing when I told him. I mean, he was upset and everything, but he tried hard not to show it.

"Don't worry, mate, we'll still see each other on a night and at weekends!"

Then I saw him, a few days later, down the shops with Matt Sanderson, when he'd told me he was at a party at his auntie's. I didn't speak to him – he didn't see me, so I thought I'd avoid the awkward conversation that was bound to come up, where he'd either have to make up a blatant lie about why he wasn't at his auntie's, or… not.

I couldn't blame him, to be honest. Who wants to have no best mate at school?

The whole 'Gemma' thing fizzled out too. Now I look back, there wasn't really much more than a bit of a verbal agreement that we were girlfriend and boyfriend. We didn't exactly go 'OUT' out. We just smiled at each other at school and she wore my jacket once.

I don't have any siblings; apparently there were 'complications' after I was born, so Mum couldn't have any more children. Which is a shame for Dad, because he'd been hoping for Juliet India Delta to come along (and little Mike Victor).

But I was totally cool with being the only child... until I had to go to Florida for ten nights and spend all that time together – just the three of us.

Although, I must say, that was when I realised that I wasn't quite as upset anymore and that I was enjoying the holiday. I also realised that I was putting on the anger and it had got into a habit that I was struggling to break.

Then we went to the Hard Rock Café...

SIX

I don't know if you've ever been to a Hard Rock Café?

They are pretty cool.

The music is great.

There are videos on big screens everywhere.

There is music memorabilia all over the walls from rock bands.

And the food is AWESOME!

We ordered a starter to share, which came on a large plate and was so big that, when the server left, bidding us, "Enjoy!" we all looked at each other and then broke out into loud laughter.

It was like a dam bursting.

You know when you've been bottling up emotion for some reason, whether it be fear, worry, or, in my case, anger, and then suddenly something breaks and all of a sudden it all comes rushing out?

Well, that's what happened.

One minute I was crying laughing, the next I was crying crying – if that makes sense?

I couldn't stop.

Mum came round to my side of the booth and hugged me, but that didn't help. At one stage I remember the server coming back – all concerned that we were in trouble and that we going to sue them for poisoning the food or something.

Eventually, I was sat outside, on a bench, with Mum and Dad. I remember the humid air and looking up at the huge, oversized, illuminated guitar, trying to catch my breath.

They both apologised and then they cried.

We must have looked completely odd, or maybe not –
we WERE in the USA after all. Land of the free, home of
over the top emotion…

And then it came to me…

Over the top.

"You'll have to change my name, Dad," I said, between
sobs.

"What? What do you mean?" he asked, stepping back a
pace, but holding onto my hand.

"After this performance, I'm not Oscar Charlie Delta
any longer… I'm Oscar Tango Tango!"

It was a simple thing, but it was like the glue that joined us
back together. We were still laughing about it on the flight
home.

SEVEN

Hysteria over, holiday over, old life over, we sat down as a family a few days later, once the clothes were all washed and put away again.

"We just want the best for you," Dad said, as he faced me across our kitchen table.

"And we realise now, that we shouldn't have treated you like a child, that we should have involved you in the decision," added Mum.

That felt good, I have to be honest.

"But your report…" Dad continued, "… was so good, that, to be honest… we felt guilty."

That surprised me.

"Guilty?"

They both looked at each other, then Dad carried on. "Yes, guilty. You see, we hadn't realised that you were quite so, well, brainy, I suppose?"

He looked a bit lost then and looked at Mum, who carried on.

"Neither of us had any support when we were at school, our parents never talked about school, they just sent us and then we left at 16 and got jobs. That was it." They looked at each other again – they'd clearly spent a lot of time talking about this.

Dad took over again, "We are really proud of you, son, and we want to give you the best possible start. Now, don't get me wrong, Brookdale was a good school and they did well for you, but the standards at Netherlea are higher and at Brookdale, you would have gone on to Horley High, whereas Netherlea send their children to Holmdale High, which is streets ahead and we just feel you'd have more opportunities."

They both sat back and I saw Dad surreptitiously grab Mum's hand.

This was it. They were waiting for my reaction.

I don't know about you, or how you would have reacted here, but I did feel like they were taking me seriously and explaining things to me like I was older. It all felt like we had crossed a bridge as a family and, (I don't know how) I just knew, that this was going to be how it was from now on.

I could have sulked and thrown several arguments back at them, but that time seemed to have passed and I felt like this was a new dawn, which I could grab hold of. I did also think that I was in a position where they owed me one and this was a great chance for me to get 'one in the bank'.

Plus, we'd all heard the stories about Horley High and the bullying – rumours were that a Year 8 boy had been stripped naked by some Year 11s and 'released' into the dinner hall recently. It had caused such a fuss that the local authority had been called in and it was all over the local paper. The Year 8 boy had had to leave because he was so embarrassed and his parents were threatening to sue the school. Holmdale, by comparison, always won all the local sports competitions and just always looked smarter when you saw them in the local park. When I thought about it, I would actually prefer to go to Holmdale… but I didn't want to reveal all my cards, there WERE deals to be done here!

I took a breath and seized the moment. "I'll be honest, I'm still a bit upset about you making the decision for me. I'm also miffed that I've lost my best mate. Added to that, I'm worried that I have absolutely no friends at all in my new school."

I looked at them both… they looked like they were going to cry… it was the Hard Rock Café all over again.

Time to add the sugar.

"But I do agree with you about Horley and Holmdale…"

They looked at each other again.

"… and I understand WHY you did this…"

They were smiling now – tentatively.

"… and I'm willing to give it a go, as long as…"

This was the moment. They had both leaned forward and were nodding along. I realised that I could ask for a lot of material things here and I'd probably get them… a PS4, a new bike, a flat-screen in my bedroom… but I was trying to be mature… the new Oscar, so I went for the winning statement. The one that they'd repeat to their friends; Dad down the Cricketers with his mates, Mum on the phone in ten minutes with Auntie Julia:

"… you keep talking to me about it all…"

They both looked at each other, with that look that either means, 'Oh, what a cute little bunny rabbit,' or, 'How proud of you we are.'

I'm hoping it was the last one.

"Of course we will, love," said Mum.

"… because I'm a bit scared, to be honest."

I thought I'd drop that one in. I mean, I was – a little – but not that much.

"That's quite understandable, son," said Dad. "I was scared when I moved jobs, I didn't know anyone, but I went in there with a positive attitude and it all worked out for the best. And now we can afford holidays in Florida and, well…"

They looked at each other again.

"We were thinking about getting you a new games console thingy, you know, like an Xbox?"

Result!

You see?

You see what happens when you don't DIRECTLY ask for something?

"Wow, really? That's amazing."

I hugged them both and they hugged back and – again – I knew something HAD changed in our relationships. I needed to keep this just like it was.

"You deserve it, son," said Mum, with tears in her eyes.

"Can I ask you one thing, Mum?" I ventured.

"Yes, of course, love."

"On my first morning, can I go in by myself? I mean, without you holding my hand, or anything?"

Mum looked unsure about this and turned to Dad for reassurance, but Dad had my back.

"I think that's a great idea, Hero!" he said. "He's growing up, Kate. Let's give him some room." Dad looked at me, wistfully, like I was about to go off to university.

Mum still looked a bit worried, but I could see that she agreed.

"Thanks… both of you," I said, thinking this would be a great closing and I stood up, smiling at them. "Well, I'm off to look online at games consoles. Maybe they have some deals on Amazon?"

"Great idea, son," said Dad. "Let us know what you find and we'll get it ordered."

And I left the room, calmly, breathing normally, but feeling quite dizzy.

Once I got into the hallway, I celebrated silently, like I'd just scored the winner at Wembley. Things had begun to look better.

FYI – ten minutes later, I heard Dad call out 'goodbye' to Mum, as he set off to the Cricketers and then Mum picked up the phone and rang her sister.

WINNING!

EIGHT

So, first day at school.

A new school.

Where I knew NOBODY!

Scary, huh?

My new teacher was a man, which Mum was excited about (they were all women at Brookdale). He was called Mr Antinori, which I was excited about.

Antinori? I wondered where he was from... India? Albania? Italy?

Mum stuck to the agreement and dropped me off in the village.

Netherlea was one of those villages with narrow roads, where two cars can't pass each other without a gesture of some kind. Some people waving, some people doing something that I'm not supposed to do – EVER, according to Mum. Sometimes, both at the same time.

She dropped me where it was safe and I walked towards the school, with all the other children and their mums and dads and grandparents. A lot of them looked twice at me. I was wearing the same uniform as them, but they didn't know me. What on earth was happening? Who was this imposter?

I should say here that the uniform was also better than Brookdale. At Brookdale, we'd had to wear a colour that my mum called 'bottle green' – which wasn't cool. My new uniform was smart: red and black, with a little logo on the jumper that was like a drawing of the school building.

None of the other children actually spoke to me, but one of the mums said, "Oh, are you the new boy then?" She smiled at me when she spoke, but then carried on walking.

I walked through the school gate and made a quick decision to turn left, as that was what the taller kids seemed to be doing.

Some kids were saying last minute goodbyes to their parents, one boy was trying (and failing) to get his mum NOT to kiss him goodbye.

"M-u-uuum!" he wailed. "Stop it!"

He looked over at me, with a look of pure terror in his eyes.

"I'm only saying goodbye, love. Don't be so silly."

"But nobody else's mums are slavvering all over them!"

"Alex, don't be daft. Anyway, nobody is watching."

I was watching, and Alex knew it.

He looked over at me, horrified, so I looked away quickly to spare him the blushes. He was about my height with short, dark, spiky hair and seemed to have a huge bag around his neck. I wondered if he'd make it to the classroom without suffocating himself.

I stopped where I was for a second and took in my surroundings: in front of me was a gaggle (not sure what the collective noun should be here, but it appears to work) of children of all shapes and sizes, all wearing red and black and most of them staring at me. The ones who weren't staring at me, were talking to others who WERE staring at me and kept stealing glances.

Behind them was an entrance door, so I guessed that I was in the right place, I just wasn't the right face.

Again, nobody appeared to want to break ranks and actually speak to me. Perhaps they were afraid.

Maybe they thought I had some strange, contagious disease? I began to contemplate making up a strange, contagious disease – after all, what did they know? My dad did say that this was an opportunity to have a fresh start. He said that, when he had changed jobs, he decided to grow a beard at the same time and felt like a different person at his new company.

I couldn't grow a beard... but I could have a strange, contagious disease. Although that probably wouldn't help me get new friends.

"My mum is SO EMBARRASSING!"

Wait, was someone talking to me?

The boy with the mum... Alex, had sidled up next to me, he still had his large bag round his neck.

Should I reply?

How do you reply to that?

I decided to look at him sympathetically, which – in case you don't know – involves raising one eyebrow and smiling with lips closed. You could try lifting one too, but DON'T, whatever you do, show any teeth. This could be misinterpreted as mocking someone.

He seemed to appreciate the look anyway, because he decided to continue standing next to me.

I wondered, briefly, if he had no friends either.

I had a moment of blind panic, when I contemplated that my first new friend had turned out to be the boy whose mother embarrassed him all the time and so none of the other kids liked him. That could be a kiss of death. I might always be known as Alex's mate and never be able to shake it off.

It didn't seem very fair; after all, I hadn't even opened my mouth to show my teeth yet, never mind spoken.

"So, you're the new boy, then?" he said, smiling at me.

WHAT... do I do now?

Perhaps I could nod, instead of speaking? Would that be rude?

He seemed nice enough.

Oh… what do I do?

"Alex!"

Someone from the crowd had saved me.

Another boy stepped forward. He was taller than me, with longer, blond hair and large, round, blue eyes. "Who's your mate?" he continued, still talking to Alex, not me.

I noticed other boys had gathered. They all appeared to be friendly. Maybe Alex did have friends.

This was so difficult.

A hand touched my shoulder and I realised it belonged to Alex, my mate?

He turned me round to face the others.

"This is the new boy. He's called…" He looked at me expectantly.

"Oscar," I replied, smiling. "My name is Oscar."

NINE

I'll be honest, the rest of the first day is a bit of a blur, but I'll try and remember what's important.

So, straight after I introduced myself, lots of boys began telling me their names. In fact, let me correct that – TOO MANY boys began telling me their names. I can't remember them, really – I can't!

The boy with the big blue eyes and blond hair was Jack – I remember that. He seemed to be a bit of a leader, the rest all seemed to look to him to make decisions. There were about seven, or eight others around, who all appeared friendly and I resolved to remember their names as soon as possible.

They all began asking me questions – at the same time. Like, "Are you from Brookdale?" and, "Do they play football there?" and, "Who's your favourite team?" It was impossible to answer them all, but, luckily, the bell ringing and a door opening, behind the crowd of kids in front of me saved me.

When I reached the door, carried along by the tide, a smiling lady, with shoulder length, dark hair and a kind face greeted me, "Morning! You must be Oscar. Come on in, love."

In I went.

In seemed to be a room, which was also a corridor and had an area for coats (I didn't have one – too warm, and I'm a boy) and packed lunches (I did have one – cheese sandwiches, no crust).

Next, I was taken along with the crowd to the classroom, where I met Mr Antinori.

This DOES stand out.

Think about what a primary school teacher looks like in your head. Next make the teacher a man. I bet you've got an image of a slim bloke with brown hair, perhaps some glasses, average height, clean-shaven, a nice shirt, maybe a jumper and a sympathetic smile? Sound about right?

This bloke was a bear of a man! Not exactly fat, but BIG. Wearing dark clothes, dark blue and/or black – not sure which. Black hair. And, most importantly... a huge beard – not long, but big, wide, bushy.

Now, when I say bushy, I don't mean scruffy, because (and you can tell I spent a lot of time examining this beard, when I should have been listening) you could see that it was neat and, well... shaped. But shaped like nothing you could expect – easily the size of his face. He had dark eyes, but they weren't frightening – they smiled when he smiled.

Well, I remember thinking, this IS going to be an interesting year.

I've no idea who I sat next to, or much about the lessons. We did do some team games and everyone seemed to be kind. Almost everyone spoke to me, even the girls, but then, Mr Antinori did make a point of telling the class that they should make me welcome and to introduce themselves to me.

So, thirty-one other children did that.

And I can remember Alex and Jack.

There was a girl that I recognised, but I don't know where from. She had what my mum calls red hair, but some people call ginger, and she also had incredible green eyes.

I remember that because I don't normally notice eyes, but these were amazing. I'd love to tell you her name, but I didn't remember.

There was a really small boy, who was very amusing. Mr Antinori had made it clear that nobody was to shout out in class and the other children clearly knew that it was best to listen to that advice because they didn't.

This was so different to Brookdale, where everyone shouted out, even Avril, who was the quietest person I've ever met.

Anyway, this small boy had a knack of making amusing comments and he did this out loud, but Mr Antinori laughed at them, so I guess that was allowed. I'd love to think of an example, but (you guessed it) I can't remember.

This one time he said something and Mr Antinori laughed this booming, deep laugh, which I felt vibrating in my stomach. I didn't know whether to be afraid, or to laugh along. I think everyone else felt the same, as there was a bit of a silence.

There was also an assembly in the hall, which was big and draughty, like halls are. We were all allowed to sit on benches at the back, while the other kids sat on the floor, which was pretty cool. The headteacher stood at the front and talked to us about rules around school and new starts. She didn't smile much, but she didn't shout. Oh, and she had black hair. That's all I can remember.

We went into the playground at breaktime and at lunch, but not onto the field – because it was wet, apparently. The playground was fun, but again most of my time was taken up by people introducing themselves to me. The rest of it was spent smiling back at all the other people in school staring at me.

It was all a bit like when you go on holiday somewhere and you can't take it all in because your senses are overloaded with new sights and sounds and smells. It was exciting and fun and I was already looking forward to going back again, but when I got in my Mum's car, I honestly couldn't remember anything with great clarity.

Parents always ask you what you've done at school that day and normally you are either a) doing something and not listening, b) about to do something and not listening, or c) listening, but you've forgotten. Sometimes, just sometimes, there's d) something that stands out, because it was really funny, or sad, or exciting, or upsetting.

This was definitely c).

When Mum stopped peppering me with questions and it got quiet, I felt a bit guilty, so I told her I'd think hard about it all and try to come up with something for round the tea table with Dad. She seemed happy with that, because she responded, "That's a good idea, love, you're probably just processing everything."

I think she was right; I was processing.

I still am.

TEN

Dad was really excited about my first day – he'd been going on about it all weekend leading up to it, so I wasn't surprised that he came home early from work.

I know I'd promised Mum that I'd think hard about it all, but my processing everything became a game of *Fortnite* and I was pretty wrapped up in it when Dad came bursting in with a big grin on his face.

"How did it go, Hero?"

Now there are two ways of handling this; I'm pretty sure I chose the wrong one. At the time, I was astounded that Dad couldn't understand that I was in the middle of a game, with thirteen minutes to play and doing well, but as soon as he'd left the room I realised that he only wanted to know if I was OK and that I'd probably upset him. The old me would have struggled to apologise, reasoning that he was my dad and he'd get over it, after all I was a kid, what was I supposed to do?

But I'd made the decision that I wasn't like that anymore, so I abandoned my game, switched everything off and followed Dad into the kitchen, where my mum was sympathising with him.

I decided it was up to me, so I went straight into it. "Sorry, Dad, I was just playing and I didn't think."

Dad turned to face me and smiled, "It's OK, son. I get it, you're decompressing after a big day."

I could see Mum breathe a sigh of relief behind him, this was clearly what she'd just told him.

"Yeah, something like that."

This new me was really working, I was the one who was building bridges. It did feel quite good.

Now if I could only think of something constructive to tell them both about my day…

"So…" Dad looked excited, "… I know someone in your class. Well, I don't *actually KNOW* them myself, but I work with someone…"

A million thoughts.

Was this good?

Would it be a nightmare, our lives intersecting like this?

This wasn't moving fast enough for my liking. "Who?" I asked, forgetting that I only actually knew two names at this point, so unless it was Alex or Jack then it wouldn't really matter.

"John Rawes."

Nothing.

It wasn't even a name I remembered hearing.

John?

There weren't any Johns in my class, were there?

"John?" I asked him. "Are you sure? I don't think there are any…"

"Oh, no. Sorry!" he began laughing. "She's not called John."

Wait, what?

"Her dad is John. The bloke I work with. Well, FOR actually. He's my boss."

OK.

That COULD be a problem. Dad works FOR someone who has a daughter in my class. Surely she wouldn't think that meant that I worked FOR her, or was beholden to her in anyway shape, or form… Would she? No, surely not. Don't be stupid, Oscar.

Dad was still smiling at me.

"And…" I prompted.

"What?"

Even Mum was getting this.

"What's HER name, love?" she asked Dad.

"Oh! Yes, sorry. Erm… I'm not sure actually."

He stood her, looking up to his left, towards our kitchen ceiling, as if her name would be magically written there.

Mum was shaking her head in exasperation. "Honestly! The men in this house! One can't remember his sandwiches."

Dad now looked down at the kitchen floor. Obviously, that was him.

"One can't remember what he did all day at his new school."

That would be me.

"And one can't remember the important part of the story he's telling."

Him again.

She was stood there now, with her arms crossed in front of her.

"I'm chasing round after both of you, making lunches, dropping off and picking up and you can't even repay me by filling me in about your day. We need another woman in this house! Someone who communicates!"

And with that, she left the room.

Dad and I were left looking around the room, guiltily. Eventually we looked at each other and Dad grimaced at me, making me feel like we were both in this together and we'd better come up with something.

"How about we go out and fetch a takeaway, or something?" I suggested.

Dad's eyes went wide. "Ooh! Great idea. I'll nip out to The Lucky Cat and get your mum some sweet and sour chicken with chips. That'll get us both back in the good books. You stay here and get the table set, put some plates in the oven and pour your mum a glass of wine."

"OK, Dad." I answered, happy that we were working together.

He picked up his keys and headed for the door, then stopped. "What do you want, Oscar?"

"I'll have that beef thing with black beans, Dad, please."

"Rice?"

"Yes please."

"Got it. Oh and son…"

"Yes, Dad."

"Have a think about some stuff you did today and I'll try and remember John's daughter's name. I'll go through the alphabet."

"OK, Dad."

ELEVEN

The next day, Tuesday, *actual* lessons began. And they didn't begin well.

Mum dropped me off.

She was happy again after the sweet and sour chicken and had just wanted to get her point across – namely, that Dad and I have memories like sieves and we should start paying attention. Dad still wasn't able to remember the name of the girl in my class, so I was hoping that maybe she'd approach me.

Well, I say I was hoping, I wanted to clear up the mystery, but wasn't exactly thrilled with the idea of any girl approaching me.

I did briefly entertain the idea that it might be the green-eyed girl, but then decided that I didn't want it to be her. There was something about her, I couldn't really explain it, but let's just say I would have been happier if she wasn't the daughter of my dad's boss.

Anyway (I'm doing that again), I didn't run into either Alex, or Jack outside school. Instead, a boy called Harry came over to talk to me.

Harry sits next to me in registration and thankfully began the conversation by saying, "Hi, remember me? Harry? I sit next to you in registration."

That helped.

Hopefully everyone in the class would be as helpful today, but I guessed not. I was just going to have to recognise the genes that my father had passed onto me and try to improve them.

Harry seemed like a good person to get to know. He told me that his mum and dad had separated during the summer, so he'd been frantically trying to remember which bedroom various clothes and school items were in. It sounded like we might have something in common.

"So, I woke up at my dad's this morning and realised that my PE kit was at my mum's, so hopefully Mr Antinori won't want to do PE today, otherwise I've got a problem." He laughed a bit at himself and his 'problem' and I wondered if he was really laughing, or whether it was to disguise something else, worry perhaps. It made me laugh anyway, so I went along with it.

It turned out that, whilst his dad lived in the village, walking distance from the school, his mum had moved out and was renting somewhere near where I live, so we made a loose arrangement to get together next time he was at his mum's – this weekend, he thought.

Everyone else started arriving, just as the bell went and there was the smiling, dark-haired, kind-faced lady at the door, saying 'Morning' to everyone in a loud, cheery voice. You couldn't help but smile back.

Mr Antinori still looked like a bear, albeit a cheerful one. My registration place was on the second row back, next to Harry. While Mr Antinori did the register, I tried to match names to faces and make mental notes to help me remember.

Will was a big kid with glasses; Jess was a thin girl with long, blond hair; Jack (as we know) has big blue eyes, Yusuf had glasses and a constant smile; Eva had long dark hair and one of those faces that gave nothing away.

Next was Carly and it turned out that she was the girl of the green eyes and red/ginger hair. I found myself gazing at her, marvelling at the way her hair had been braided (or was it plaited?). It was remarkably organised, how it was weaved together – certainly not something that she could have done by herself – could she? No, surely her mum would have done it. But it must have taken…

"OSCAR!"

I suddenly realised that Mr Antinori was talking to me. What had I been doing? Surely I hadn't been staring at the green-eyed, I mean... Carly?

Everything in the room had stopped and the whole class was staring at me.

Was I supposed to say something?

"Now you've woken up from your daydream, Mr Delta," Mr Antinori was saying, in a sarcastic, yet semi-serious voice, "could we possibly establish whether you are here? At least in body, if not in mind."

"Erm, yes. Sorry," I managed.

Was I in trouble? Mum and Dad had warned me about catching the teacher's attention for the wrong reason early on, in case he formed an impression of me. Had I ruined that?

"Where were you, Mr Delta?" he continued.

I didn't think I could answer that, so managed to croak out a... "I'm not sure, Mr Antinori."

Others were leaning into each other around me, whispering to each other about the new boy. How embarrassing.

"Well, you definitely weren't on this planet. Perhaps another world?"

Then a voice piped up, the same voice that had managed to make people, including Mr Antinori, laugh yesterday. Remember that little guy that I mentioned. I'm pretty sure I liked him.

Liked.

Until now.

"I think he was on planet Carly, Mr Antinori," he called out.

There was a very definite pause. Only for a millisecond, but it was there. In that pause I could hear my own breathing, very loud in my ears, almost vibrating. Maybe it was my heart beating also.

Then the whole class erupted into laughter.

What a nightmare.

The thing was, if it had been targeted at someone else in the class, I probably would have been laughing and it was only that thought which made me able to get through it. That and the fact that this was the new, sensible me, who could deal with anything. I reasoned that this would die down. Mr Antinori had already silenced the class and, after giving me a brief nod and a smile, which I read as, 'I hope you're OK, but you brought that on yourself,' he continued with the register.

Obviously, the rest of the class were now aware that they could be next, so everyone concentrated and we got though it pretty quickly.

Maybe everyone had now forgotten?

Surely by break lots of other things would have gone on, so that it would be in the past?

"Right, everyone," began Mr Antinori. "Now we are going to our maths places. Hopefully you remember those from our little induction yesterday?"

I think I did.

"You will need a sharp pencil and a ruler and Mrs Johnson will give out the maths books. Off you go."

I grabbed my pencil and a ruler from my drawer and stood up, looking around the room.

Harry next to me gave me a little smile of understanding, as he stood up too. "See you in a bit, mate," he said and turned to head off to his chair.

I remembered that my seat was on the back row for maths, not on the middle, but not on the end, so I made my way towards the back of the room. I passed Alex, who nodded at me, so I nodded back. He didn't seem to be smiling, so he wasn't laughing at me.

Maybe everyone really had already forgotten?

People were milling around trying to get to their maths places, before Mr Antinori started to get annoyed; this just made it harder to get where I wanted to go. I started to doubt whether I was going the right way.

I didn't want to be in trouble twice in the same morning
– that would not look good.

Then I remembered.

I was definitely on the left side of the room.

Not the last seat, next to the wall, but next to that.

The crowd was thinning out now, as people found their
places and sat down, there was only one place left at the
back and that was mine.

Next to…

Carly.

Who was staring at me, like she wanted to kill me.

Excellent.

TWELVE

Once I'd sat down and Mrs Johnson (the dark-haired, kind-faced lady, who was no longer at the door) had given me my maths book, I sneaked a sideways glance at Carly, just in time to catch her looking away.

I could feel the anger coming off her, like a heat.

My Mum's sister, Auntie Julia is a redhead – that's what mum calls her. Dad has often brought up the topic of their temperaments matching their hair colour – not when she's in the room; he wouldn't dare do that. Mum has told us stories of arguments from when they were kids and how her temper would get her into trouble and how you should never make decisions when you are emotional, using her sister as an example. Usually at Christmas, later in the day, after a few drinks, Auntie Julia's mood will change dramatically and she can get quite shouty. That's when I leave the adults to it and disappear to watch TV. Normally it's the next morning when Dad and Mum start having the chat about redheads and their temperaments.

Anyway, I couldn't go in the other room to watch TV, as Mr Antinori wouldn't be as forgiving as my parents, and it was kind of my fault, so I was just going to have to get on with it.

"You are *supposed* to be opening your book," Carly hissed at me, without turning her head.

I realised that I'd been off in another world again and that all around me were busy with getting their maths books set up for the lesson. Mr Antinori was demonstrating the presentation that he expected, "… and I do NOT want any crossing out! A simple 'x' next to any mistakes will suffice, then you can continue next to it."

I sneaked a look at Carly's book and saw she had written the date at the top of the first page, so I did the same.

"Thanks," I whispered back to her.

I got a grunt in response.

As we were all writing the learning objective down – neatly, with a SHARP pencil – I wondered why I was starting to daydream all of a sudden. I'd never done it before.

Was it the green eyes?

It couldn't be, could it? Green eyes?

Was I being hypnotised by them?

No, surely not… it must be just the new school. But, I was OK yesterday.

Oh no, it was the green eyes, wasn't it?

"You've written the *wrong thing!*"

What?

"What?" I whispered back, turning to look at Carly's book.

She had her finger underneath the learning objective and was gesturing at the words.

I couldn't understand what she meant, so looked back at my own book.

But that just brought a new reaction, as she began tapping furiously at her page. The tapping was getting more frenetic, but I was lost. I glanced at her face, to find her teeth clamped tightly together, her nose wrinkled at the end and her eyes bulging out.

Scary!

I then turned back towards the front of the room with, what I can only expect was, a look of puzzlement on my face.

Just in time to see my teacher stop what he was doing and turn his head.

"Is everything OK back there?"

Mr Antinori was looking at us both.

In fact, the whole class was looking at us both. Some, I noticed, had sly smiles on their faces.

Neither of us spoke.

"You look puzzled, Mr Delta," he offered. "Is something confusing you?"

"Erm," I managed.

"And you, Miss Davies, seem to be adding a kind of percussion to my lesson. Are you expecting some singing?"

"No, Mr Antinori. Sorry. I was just trying to point out to Oscar that he had written the wrong learning objective."

Sweetness and light.

This girl was something else. The anger was clearly turned up to eleven next to me, a white-hot fury heating the whole corner of the classroom, but she was able to mask this and sound like she was stroking puppies, like butter wouldn't melt in her mouth.

I was quite scared, but I couldn't decide who I was most scared of: Mr Antinori – bear of a teacher, with a huge beard, or the ten-year-old girl next to me with the most amazing green eyes.

I was doing it again, wasn't I?

I was daydreaming.

"I said," began Mr Antinori, in a voice much louder than before, "what HAVE you written, Oscar?"

I just wanted to start the day again.

What had I written?

What WAS the learning objective?

"Erm…" I replied. For the SECOND time.

I looked at the board – where it read quite clearly, 'LO – To understand place value.'

"Never mind, I'll come and look for myself," said Mr Antinori, heading straight for my desk.

I looked down at my book, feeling the stares from the rest of the room burning into me.

What had I written?

The date was correct.

My presentation was good.

I was just getting to the line underneath when a large hand snatched my book away from me.

"Interesting learning objective, Mr Delta, very interesting indeed."

The room was deathly silent.

Everybody, including me, wanted to know what I had written.

"Oh… no," came out as a quiet breath next to me.

Obviously, Carly knew what I had written and it sounded like it was something that was going to embarrass her.

Like she had already been embarrassed once before this morning.

I was doing a great job at making new friends, wasn't I?

"I think we'll have a chat at break time, Mr Delta."

And with that, Mr Antinori closed my maths book and placed it down in front of me, before heading back to the front of the room.

THIRTEEN

"To understand *green eyes*."

Mr Antinori leaned back against the desk behind him, as he looked down at me.

I looked down at my desk, in despair, embarrassment, shame, shall I keep going?

"What are you doing, Oscar?"

I have to say here, I was surprised. He wasn't angry – at least he didn't *seem* angry. He appeared to be on my side, which confused me. At Brookdale the teachers always shouted at children who were kept in at break and sometimes they got sent to the headteacher's office. That had never happened to me though. And here I was... on my second day!

I decided to take the same route as I was taking at home: the new me, standing up and facing the issues head on.

So I looked up at him.

"I honestly don't know, Mr Antinori. I've never been like this before. I'm sorry. It won't happen again."

"But can you guarantee that, Oscar? It does seem like you are under a spell."

Under a spell?

Maybe I was.

I didn't know what to add, so I just stayed quiet, in the hope that what I'd said was enough.

"I've read your reports from Brookdale," he continued. "and spoken on the phone with a Mrs Barker, who taught you last year, and you seem like a really capable lad, who works hard in class. She said I'd never have a moment's problem with you and that they were sorry you had left."

I put my head down again, looking at my maths book, where I'd rubbed 'green eyes' out carefully and written 'place value' over it.

Mr Antinori tapped my page. "Your maths is clearly very good and I've got high hopes for you this year Oscar. But…"

He let the 'but' dangle, as he stood up and walked away from my desk. Then he turned to face me again and stepped back towards me.

"… you can't get *distracted* by other members of the class."

It was clear what he was talking about.

"No matter… how much you are captivated by their looks."

With this he smiled. It was a smile that said, 'I understand' and, at that moment, I decided that this was going to be the best school year I'd had. That this new teacher was someone who cared about me, who wanted me to succeed, but understood that I was just a person, who could make mistakes.

I decided that I was going to work hard for Mr Antinori and make him proud of me.

"Am I going to have to split you and *green eyes* up?" he asked, with the same smile.

I smiled back at him and replied, "No, you don't have to. I won't let you down again, Mr Antinori."

He nodded his head several times, before saying, "I know you won't Oscar. Get yourself out for some break."

FOURTEEN

I didn't feel too much like going outside and exposing myself to the inevitable mickey-taking, so I hung around in the area outside the classroom, ducking into the boys' toilets, when I heard Mr Antinori coming out of the class.

When I thought it was reasonable that the coast was clear, I came back out, only to find three girls from my class waiting for me.

I recognised one of them as the thin girl, with long, blond hair – Jess, but I didn't know the other two, except by sight. Jess was stood to my left, with a smile on her face, which didn't exactly seem like she was there to sympathise.

The girl on the right had dark, brown hair in a ponytail on top, round, brown eyes and a skirt, which looked a tad on the short side, if you asked me. She wore the same smile.

The leader was obviously the one in the middle. Although she was as short as Jess, she had a bit of a 'don't mess with me attitude' going on and looked at me as if I was a piece of dirt. I'd not come across someone like her at Brookdale, but I knew the type: rich parents, spoilt, thought everyone should bow down before her – like her two stooges were doing.

She wasn't smiling.

I didn't really have time for this. My day hadn't exactly been a roaring success so far and, whilst I'd just promised Mr Antinori that I wasn't going to be any further trouble, I wasn't going to be put in my place by someone like this.

Clearly nobody was going to speak first, so I decided to open with, "What?"

The two stooges, Jess and Short Skirt, both looked at Posh Girl for leadership.

Posh Girl continued to stare at me for a moment, then began to smile, opening her mouth to reveal teeth held in place by a brace, which looked like it had jewels on it. She had extremely clean, tidy blond hair, which was held in place by a silver and black hair band with a little bow on one side of her head. I really didn't like her.

I know, I know, you aren't supposed to judge people before you know them and she might be really lovely, but she obviously had a much higher opinion of herself than she did of anybody else and that's just not right.

Added to that, she STILL wasn't talking.

"Helloooo?" I said, over-exaggerating the 'o' while wobbling my head side to side. "Do you speak English?"

This got a result.

Posh Girl put one hand on her hip, closed her mouth and pouted, looking up to one side, as if one of us had used the wrong fork for their starter.

The stooges didn't seem to know what to do. They were simultaneously looking at each other, then back at Posh Girl; clearly this didn't happen very often.

I wasn't going outside, but I wasn't standing here, so I barged through them, heading for the door, as if I *was* going outside.

I didn't *exactly* push them aside, but it did cause them to knock into each other and Short Skirt got the worst of it.

She span around on one ankle and lost her balance, tumbling to the floor, legs all over the place, skirt no longer doing its job.

And that was when Short Skirt became Pink Knickers.

Jess dashed to her aid, looking back at me like I'd just murdered her hamster. Pink Knickers got to her feet, already in floods of tears and ran into the girls' toilet, followed by Jess, looking back at me one more time for effect, just in case I hadn't realised that I'd killed Mr Cuddles.

Posh Girl whirled around to face me.

"Wait until my father hears about this!"

I don't know about you, but when someone comes out with a statement like that, I think it deserves a sarcastic response.

So I came out with, "Why? Does he wear pink knickers too?"

Which, on reflection, wasn't ideal, but I was proud of it at the time.

Instead of looking annoyed (as I expected), or angry (which was understandable), or even upset (again, a possibility), Posh Girl just looked, well... victorious.

I didn't get it.

Then she walked right up to me, standing in front of me, so that I could see the tiny pimple on the side of her upturned nose and said, "No, but he's your dad's boss and I think he'll want to talk to your dad about his son's naughty behaviour in class, as well as the way he treats girls, pushing them over. Don't you?"

Maybe I should have gone outside after all?

FIFTEEN

I don't need to tell you what happened next.

Obviously, Mr Antinori came back to class and found three hysterical girls – one of them legitimately upset and two others putting on a heck of an act – who wanted to fill him in on an incident at break time, when Oscar came storming out of the toilets and pushed through them, knocking Daisy over.

Mr Antinori looked at me with a resigned expression, which I couldn't blame him for. I didn't attempt to interrupt the drama in front of me, as I knew that wouldn't get me anywhere and, besides, I was too busy wondering how I could speak to my dad before his boss did.

I managed to get through the English lesson, sat next to a chubby lad called Ben, who seemed more interested in the contents of his nose than the general opinion of the new boy and his antics today.

Mr Antinori had simply told me that I was to spend lunch inside on the corridor, eating my sandwiches while staring at a display about e-Safety, which *wasn't* very interesting after the third read.

One of the lunchtime supervisors (Miss Whittell) had checked in with me a couple of times. She was really, REALLY friendly and didn't seem bothered that I was a criminal.

Ten minutes before the afternoon bell, Mr Antinori sat down next to me with a sigh.

"Do you think you can manage to get through this afternoon without upsetting any more girls in my class, Oscar?"

I turned to face him.

Again, he didn't look angry. Just disappointed.

"I'm sorry Mr Antinori. I know I said that I wouldn't let you down again, but it really wasn't my fault…"

"Stop!" he said. He didn't quite shout it, but he definitely raised his voice a bit.

I think he realised too, because he looked around the corridor to see if anyone else had heard him, but there was only the two of us there.

He continued in a much quieter voice, "I don't want to hear it. I know very well what Isabella-Jane Rawes is like. I've had experience of her antics in the past. I just hoped that you might keep your head down after what we discussed at break."

I thought about telling him exactly what had happened and even opened my mouth to begin, but he just held up his hand, so I closed it again.

"There's a spare desk in the classroom, Oscar. We have too many, so we only use it occasionally. I'm going to sit you in it this afternoon, then you can't get into any more trouble."

"OK, Mr Antinori, I understand."

He smiled again. Not a wide-open mouth smile of happiness. More of a 'let's get through it together' smile.

Then he stood up.

"Come on. Let's get today over with and then start again tomorrow in your normal place. Let's just write this off as a bad day and never talk about it again."

"Yes, Mr Antinori. Thanks."

I stood up and followed him through school with my sandwich box. When we got to the classroom the bell rang.

45

He pointed out my new desk and I began to swap my drawer over.

"Oh, and Oscar."

"Yes, Mr Antinori."

He lowered his voice again and looked at me like he was letting me into a secret.

"Be careful around Izzy. Most of the girls are wise to her, but boys aren't armed with the same... capabilities."

Even though I'd let him down, even though I seemed to be trying my best to ruin his day, even though I'd disrupted the relationships in his class, I truly believed Mr Antinori had my back.

"Thank you, Mr Antinori. I'll try."

He walked back to his desk and turned around. "In fact, be careful around all of the girls! You are new, so that makes you interesting. Everyone is measuring you up and you seem to be causing quite a fuss. Try to be invisible for a bit, while it dies down, eh?"

At that moment, the classroom door opened and the class all returned, most of them looking over at me, knowingly. The new boy's in trouble!

Brilliant.

I just wanted this day to end.

SIXTEEN

"Pink knickers?"

I just looked at Dad. I think my face said it all.

"Pink knickers, Oscar? You suggested that my *boss* wears pink knickers? To his *daughter*?"

Dad looked stressed.

He still had his jacket on and was still carrying his bag, which he was waving around in the air as he demonstrated how upset he was. He'd literally come straight up to my bedroom from walking in the door.

I didn't want to add to his stress level.

I didn't *want to…*

But I did.

I think I'd just had enough. So I did what everyone does… I took it out on my family.

"I didn't actually *say* that he wore pink knickers," I replied.

"Don't split hairs, you know what you said."

This made me laugh… so I did. "Ha! And you do? You have no idea what happened, Dad. You weren't there!"

Dad dropped his bag and made a noise that expressed his frustration and sounded a bit like, "Ruuuuuurrrgh!"

I understood him. I felt frustrated too, so I stood up, to make a point.

Which could have been seen as threatening behaviour and wasn't going to defuse the situation.

"Sit yourself back down. I'm not finished with you yet. You have NO IDEA how embarrassing it is for your boss to confront you over your son's behaviour in school. Getting in trouble at break, pushing girls over and then making insulting comments about people's parents!"

Wow. She really HAD told him everything, hadn't she? What a cow!

I stood there (I hadn't sat back down), shaking my head at it all.

"And DON'T you shake your head at me. Do you know the trouble that you have caused?"

That was it!

"It wasn't MY fault, OK? YOU weren't there. I didn't know she was your boss's daughter. YOU sent me to this *stupid* school, with *stupid* girls, who get you into trouble, with their *stupid* green eyes and their *stupid,* posh attitudes and their *stupid,* smiley friends!"

Obviously, none of this made actual sense. I was rambling.

"DON'T you raise your voice to me, young man!" replied Dad, with a vein popping out of his forehead. "You are grounded!"

"Grounded? Ha! GOOD! So, you mean I won't be able to play with all of my new *friends* from my new school. BIG DEAL!"

I didn't realise I was shouting, until Mum came bursting in. "What is all of this noise? What's the matter?"

I would have stormed out, except I had nowhere to storm to. I was in my own bedroom, with both parents between me and the door.

So I turned round, to face my window.

This is where I would have normally cried.

The old me that is.

The new me realised that crying (whilst relieving some of the stress) wouldn't actually achieve anything. Besides, I hadn't done anything wrong… well… I had, but it hadn't really been my fault.

Had it?

Could I have avoided it? Could I have walked away from Isabella-Banana, or whatever her name was?

I suppose I could have.

But then, would she have won? People (especially *girls*) like that rely on power and manipulation. If they know that you are afraid of them, then they'll play with that. Isabella-Banana, with her 'my dad is your dad's boss' and 'I'm the boss of you' attitude couldn't be allowed to win otherwise my life would be a misery. Before I knew it, I'd be having to carry her bags around and do her homework for her.

No, thank you!

And Carly Green Eyes – what was her last name again? – with her green eyes and, well…

"OSCAR!"

I was doing it again.

What WAS wrong with me? Was I always going to be like this?

I turned back round to face my parents, who looked both agitated and deeply concerned at the same time.

Then I took a deep breath.

"Dad, I'm sorry, OK, but I'm having a very stressful time."

Mum started wringing her hands and looked like she would have hugged me if angry Dad wasn't standing right next to her.

I carried on before either of them spoke. "Can I tell you about my day? Then you can either give me some advice, or lock me in the basement for a week, whichever you think is most suitable."

SEVENTEEN

In my new spirit of honesty and maturity at home (I hadn't quite managed it at school yet), I was completely and utterly honest with them both.

I even told them about my daydreaming, which looked like it was worrying them both, then I mentioned Carly and her green eyes and they both looked at each other in that way that adults do, when they think that they are sharing information that only they understand. They smiled at me then and Dad actually nodded his head, like he was proud of me.

I didn't know whether all kids in Year 6 go through what I was currently going through, but it was very strange.

Almost exciting and incredibly annoying at the same time. If that makes sense?

Anyway, the outcome was that we sat around the table, eating a really good chilli and laughing about it.

Even Dad was laughing about his boss and saying that he didn't think he'd be able to look at him again, without wondering whether he *was* wearing pink knickers.

There was the usual parental advice. Although Dad was very happy about Carly, he recommended 'playing it cool' with her. Apparently, what this entailed was that I thought about her like she was just one of my friends and got that attitude in my head, like she's just another boy and so treat her like that.

In his incredibly wide experience (my words, not his), he advised that this would have two effects: one – I wouldn't get in any more trouble with my teacher, and two – she would find me irresistible!

Mum was NOT happy with this, I can tell you.

In fact, she went quiet for a while.

The end result was that we all went to bed on good terms and I was happy that:

a) This horrible day was over
b) I'd been completely honest with Mum and Dad about what had gone on
c) Mum and Dad seemed to back me up on the decisions I'd taken.

Now all we needed to do was get through the rest of the week.

EIGHTEEN

And, I'm happy to report that I did just that.

When the bell went at the end of Friday afternoon, I had a big grin on my face, I can tell you.

Mr Antinori stopped me on the way out of class and congratulated me, sarcastically, on three days of school without upsetting any girls. We both laughed and it felt good.

"Have a great weekend, Mr Antinori," I told him.

"And you too, Oscar. Are you doing anything nice?"

I told him I wasn't sure what was going on, but that we normally go to see my gran and he said that, amazingly, he was also going to see his gran.

I wondered how old his gran was? I guessed that she must be in her eighties at least. I mean, Mr Antinori looked like he was in his forties, about Dad's age, so that would make his parents *at least* sixty.

I didn't think it was polite to ask, so I just told him he should take her a cake. We *always* take my gran a cake; she loves cake. And, to be fair, so do we. It's just a good excuse for us all to eat cake and not feel bad about it. That's what Dad says anyway.

"Thanks, Oscar, that's a great idea. I'll do just that."

I didn't SKIP out of school, but I could have.

What started out as a disaster had turned into a really good week and I was feeling optimistic again.

But I was under no illusion... things could change very quickly.

I'd managed to avoid Isabella-Banana and her stooges, only passing them in the classroom. She (Isabella-Banana) had attempted to give me a 'look' on the first couple of times, but I'd looked away, like I didn't even see her, and she seemed to have stopped doing it now.

Maths lessons sat next to Carly had similarly worked out well. I'd taken Dad's advice and treated her like I treat boys and the effects (in case you are interested) were:

1 – I wasn't getting into trouble for anything, and

2 – she was starting to talk to me about things other than maths and she had actually laughed at something I'd said in class, while we were working out a problem.

I wasn't going to bring this up at home though. I didn't want Dad to start giving me more advice that could upset Mum.

Another good thing, which may, or may not, be linked to the above, is that I hadn't been daydreaming AT ALL! I wasn't sure whether this meant that the daydreaming was in the past, so I was trying hard not to be complacent, but still being aware of things.

At home, Dad hadn't mentioned his boss at all, so I could only hope that everything was now OK there and he wasn't about to lose his job because of his terrible son. I'll be honest and say that I hadn't asked him about it, in the hope that it had gone away.

So, fingers crossed.

One week down…

Thirty-eight to go.

NINETEEN

Nothing of any interest happened in the next few days at all.

Well, nothing that's worth me writing down here anyway.

We'd seen Gran and shared most of a Victoria sponge cake and then watched an episode of *Pointless* with celebrities on. Well, I say celebrities – I hadn't actually heard of any of them, but Mum liked one of them from a soap opera. My gran loves *Pointless* and the main reason for that is that tall bloke, Richard Osman. She says he's 'fit', which makes me shudder and probably isn't appropriate for someone my gran's age, but then my grandpa has been dead for about twenty-nine years, so her having some kind of long range crush on a tall bloke from the TV is preferable to her having an 'actual' boyfriend, who she might want to take to nightclubs.

You're probably laughing, but knowing my gran, she probably would want to take a boyfriend to nightclubs.

And that's just wrong... on so many levels.

Mr Antinori made a point of telling the entire class that he'd taken his grandma a chocolate cake, which made me very proud. He then made me even more proud – and little embarrassed – by announcing that it had been *my* suggestion. All the eyes in the room had turned to me for the right reasons this time. He'd gone on to tell us all that his gran was ninety-eight.

NINETY-EIGHT!

That's old!

Apparently she hadn't spoken much in the past year or so and got tired very easily, but the introduction of a chocolate cake had put, what Mr Antinori called, a 'spring in her step' – which (Mrs Barker would be happy to know) is a metaphor.

Carly had gone out of her way to approach me in the playground that lunchtime to tell me that she thought that what I'd done was 'sweet'. I temporally forgot about Dad's advice on how to be around her and lapsed back into the day two Oscar. My mind went completely blank and I just stared at her with, what I *hoped* was a smile on my face. She wandered off shortly afterwards and I caught sight of Archie – the small boy, who was still making the sarcastic comments in class, but thankfully not about me. He was smiling over at me, knowingly.

I wondered if he was logging the exchange for future material.

I can only look back and wonder if it was seeing Carly in an unfamiliar surrounding that made me so tongue-tied?

I know, *I know,* the school playground isn't really unfamiliar, but it did seem that boys spoke only to boys and girls to girls. It wasn't like that at Brookdale, but I was becoming accustomed to the fact that Netherlea was completely different and I was trying hard to fit in with these new customs and not stand out like a sore thumb.

Other than that, all was harmonious in the class.

Until the strange occurrences of Thursday.

TWENTY – The Strange Occurrences of Thursday

Remember I mentioned before that I thought I'd seen Carly before, but I couldn't remember where from and what she was called?

Well...

Normal people go to get their hair cut BEFORE they start back at school in September. *We* couldn't claim to be normal people because *our* hairdresser was on holiday in Minorca until Thursday.

Our hairdresser is a friend of my mum's, called Penny, and we've been going to her since forever.

She doesn't have an actual shop – or 'salon' as they are called by everyone else who goes to get their hair cut – oh no, we go to Penny's house.

Now I don't know whether this is technically legal and I'm not actually sure how much money Mum pays Penny, but the routine is: we go to Penny's and sit in her kitchen, Mum has a cup of tea and sometimes I get some Ribena type stuff, that's not actually Ribena. I will say here that Penny doesn't have any children of her own and that's probably why I have some weak blackberry-tasting water. Penny doesn't have time for children of her own, because she's always on holiday and if you ever meet Penny you will see the evidence of that, because she is extremely brown – which can NOT be good for you.

I'm side-tracking again here, but Mrs Barker told us last year (and this has stuck with me) that our children will probably be astonished to hear that their grandparents used to actively go OUT IN THE SUN and try to BURN THEMSELVES.

When you think about it, she's right.

Why do people do that?

Mrs Barker says that somewhere someone decided in the 1970s that you looked healthy if you had a suntan. Stevie (whose mum is a travel agent) said that it was probably a travel company and Mrs Barker told him that she was sure he was right.

Anyway, that stuck with me and now every time I go for my haircut, I marvel at how odd Penny looks; she looks completely unnatural and not very healthy. I've spoken to mum about this and she says that Penny will look like a ninety-year-old when she's fifty – which can't be good.

ANYWAY (we're here again), I normally sit in the kitchen and watch Penny's flat-screen TV, while Mum gets her hair cut and then it's my turn. I say 'normally' because I don't *always* do that and *as soon as I sat in the chair in the kitchen* I realised why.

Can you guess?

If you can, then you're very good, because I haven't given you any clues yet.

As I said, Penny doesn't have any children... HOWEVER she does have a Niece. And this Niece is 'about' my age and since I've been coming to get my hair cut here, which (as I said) is for EVER, sometimes Penny's Niece is at her house and sometimes I play with her in the back garden, or the garage, because Penny has a table tennis table and she lets me use it.

Can you guess now?

If not, then you aren't following this story very well.

Literally AS SOON AS I SAT IN THE CHAIR everything snapped into place.

AND... as soon as it snapped into place, Penny said, "Oh Oscar, Carly is upstairs. Why don't you go and get her down here and you can go play table tennis or something?"

WOW!

Now, you'd think that I would have realised that that's where I knew Carly from, wouldn't you?

But sometimes you just need to be in the right place for things to click into place. And, to be fair to me, I hadn't seen her in the last year or so.

So now, here I was, going upstairs to surprise Carly.

As I said, we'd got on quite well for the past few days (since the Learning Objective incident and the daydreaming in registration incident before that), but I wasn't sure how she'd be feeling about me stalking her to her bedroom at her auntie's house.

So... I knocked... gently.
    So gently, that there was no response.

So, I knocked again, a bit more forcefully.
    And again, there was no response.

I stood there for a moment, wondering whether this was actually happening and then knocked for a third time. This time I knocked so loudly that the door actually shook and Penny shouted up from downstairs, "You'll have to go in, love, she'll have her headphones on!"

Great, now I was sneaking up on her by breaking and entering. There was no way that this could end well.

I slowly pulled down on the golden (not *real* gold) handle and pushed the door open.

Again, there was no reaction, but I could actually hear the repetitive beat of music. I stepped forward, putting one foot into the bedroom, which had a blue carpet – in case you wondered and then the rest of my body followed.

As soon as my head was around the door, I could see Carly.

Now... this really was getting scary. I quickly took stock.

I was a ten-year old boy, who had been in trouble TWICE in the week previous to this moment for *essentially* fancying the girl that I was facing.

I was standing in the bedroom that she was using at her auntie Penny's home.

She was lying on the bed in this bedroom, facing the other way, with headphones on, relaxing, with no idea AT ALL that her privacy was being invaded because she was listening to what sounded like George Ezra.

What would you have done?

Quickly, think about it. You can't take all day and come back to me, it has to be an immediate decision, because that's what I had.

The way I saw it, I could:
1) Leave the room and then the house and find a new hairdresser.
2) Tap her on the shoulder, which would involve me leaning ON THE BED, WHICH SHE WAS LYING IN.
3) Walk slowly further into the room until she noticed me.

The first one was out, because that would just be odd, but the other two were bound to lead to me making her jump and – remember she has red hair (Auntie Julia!) – dealing with the consequences.

In the end, I did none of them and instead decided to do something that was completely out of character for me…

I jumped.

Yes… that's right. You heard me.
    I jumped.
    Not on the bed, you understand, because that would mean that I'd have to leave Netherlea School and would probably involve a visit to the local police station too.

No.
    I jumped into her line of vision.

AND… I didn't just jump; I did that thing when you raise your hands by your sides and actually WAVED with both hands.

If you are going to do something embarrassing, then you might as well do it whole-heartedly.

The thing was… it didn't exactly work out as I thought. Not that I had thought long and hard about this, you understand. And the reason why was, she had her eyes closed.
    Yes, she was lost in a world of her own, probably imaging herself standing alongside George Ezra as he sang to her personally.

So the actual action didn't have the reaction that I (and you) expected – I will say here that Mrs Barker would probably have liked the effect of 'actual action' with 'reaction' – but I'm getting side-tracked again.
    The thing was… the effect of me landing and the vibration it caused, led to her opening her eyes and finding yours truly stood in front of her, in a star shape, with wavy hands.

Cool, huh?

What do you think her actual reaction was?

TWENTY-ONE – The Strange Occurrences of Thursday (Part II)

I could leave you dangling here and start talking about something else, like my dad's brother Matt, who has a bar in a shed in his garden and loves it more than anything in the world – including his family – but NOT his favourite football team, Branley United, who seem to lose more often than not, but he's convinced that one day, ONE DAY… they'll be back in the top flight.

But I won't, because that would be cruel.

First Carly threw off the headphones, then she backed up against the headboard of the bed and the wall and while she was doing all of this she shouted, "WHAT THE HELL!"

Her eyes were massively wide and she looked quite frightened. She had actually lifted both hands up to the side of her head, which made her look like that strange painting, The Scream.

What probably made things even more frightening – and possibly disturbing – was the fact that I was still waving both hands… I'm not sure why.

I don't really know why I was doing any of this. In fact, ever since I'd opened the bedroom door I'd been operating as if programmed by a foreign intelligence service. I certainly didn't feel like I was in control of my own actions.

Weird, huh?

"What the ACTUAL HELL are you doing here, Oscar?"

I decided now was the time to stop waving. I can remember making that decision, but I didn't just stop dead (because that would be weird, right? As opposed to everything else that was happening here), no, I slowed them down to a stop, like a song fading out before it ends. I'm not sure that Carly noticed, but I know I was concentrating on this small detail and it was helping me stall for time, while I made my next momentous decision.

"Hello? Oscar?"

"Your auntie sent me upstairs," I whined, in a whiny voice.
So all the stalling for time hadn't helped at all. Why couldn't I have just spoken normally?

"What? Why?" she said, looking as confused as anybody possibly could look. "What are you actually doing at my auntie's home?"

"IS EVERYTHING OK UP THERE?" shouted Penny from downstairs, interrupting the confusion in the room.
    Good question.
    "YEAH!" Carly shouted back, leaning forwards a bit and facing towards the door. Then she turned back to me, eyebrows furrowed above those green eyes.

Now I was confused. Did she really not know? Had she forgotten as well as me?
    "You mean you don't know? You don't remember me?"
    "I remember you as the odd boy who sits next to me in maths and is a potential stalker."
    Fair comment, I couldn't argue with that, but a little rude.
    "That's nice. Thanks," I said instead and probably looked a little hurt.

I was stood in front of the window now – minus the jazz hands, looking crestfallen. Once again, I felt like I'd got into a situation that I hadn't really caused, which had led to me looking foolish.

Was this what being older was going to be like? Being aware of my own stupidity, but unable to prevent it happening repeatedly... like that film, *Groundhog Day* that mum made me watch with her at Easter when we stayed in that Premier Inn at Scarborough?

I turned to the door and started to walk towards it, but she stopped me, holding out her arm, her hand touching my chest.

"Wait... Oscar, sorry. You just startled me, that's all."

I looked down at her hand, which was still touching my chest. Did she *know* she was touching me? I felt a bit strange, it wasn't an unpleasant sensation, but I felt like I was doing something wrong, when I wasn't the one doing the touching. Maybe I felt guilty for liking the fact that she was touching me? As I say, life was getting to be a nerve-wracking thing.

I decided to ignore it and use my dad's strategy.

"Well, I didn't know what to do. I knocked three times. Then your auntie shouted up that I should come in and, well, you know what happened then."

"OK, OK... sorry, I shouldn't have shouted," she said, STILL touching my chest. Then, just as suddenly, she seemed to realise that she was doing it and removed her hand as if it was touching a burning oven.

"Oh. Sorry!" Now it was her turn to look horrified. And – I was happy to see – she had turned a bright shade of red. I was now on top.

Time to use the strategy that I'd been practising at home.

"No, don't worry," I said, lifting my right arm in a gesture that was meant to mean that all was OK, with my palm flat, facing towards her, but somehow I ended up grabbing hold of her hand as she was removing hers.

Now things were really awkward.

We both faced each other, hands linked in a fashion that I'm sure has never been practiced before – my ring finger wrapped around her index finger and my middle finger laced between her index finger and thumb.

We looked at each other, both with eyes as close to 'on stalks' as it is possible to be, neither daring to move their hand first.

She looked down at our hands, then I did.

Then an incredible thing happened.

She started laughing.

TWENTY-TWO – The Strange Occurrences of Thursday (Part III)

Now, you are aware of my irrational – some would say – *obsession* with Carly's eyes and the thought I'd given to her hair colour.

Those two things should be enough.

But… her laugh.

Magical properties, like a sing song it was infectious and immediately we were both laughing, then – before I knew it – somehow, we weren't doing the bizarre hand grasping and we were both sat on the bed laughing.

The whole situation was defused and all was good.

But clearly it would need some deep thought at a later date.

It turned out that Carly had forgotten the whole playing together as little kids also (or so she said) and didn't remember me at all (not sure I'm buying that, but not going to argue).

She asked me about my old school, so I told her about Stevie (but not Gemma!) and Mrs Barker and we discussed things that were different.

She filled me in on some things about my new classmates, stories about things that had gone on in previous years, like apparently Archie – the small, sarcastic kid – had a really bad year last year. His dad, who was a fireman, had been killed in an incident at work and he'd gone quiet afterwards, hardly speaking at all. Carly said that she thought that's why teachers let him shout out in class now, because anything was better than nothing, right?

Poor Archie.

I didn't really know anything about him – I hadn't actually ever spoken to him. He was just this kid in class that said stuff to make people laugh.

I made a resolution to get to know him in the next week or so.

Pretty soon after that, Penny shouted me down for my trim and more or less straight after that we had to go, as it was a 'school night'.

Penny and Mum suggested that – as we'd got on so well together, we should all get together soon and maybe go out for lunch (a 'playdate' they called it, looking at each other, like adults do when they think we kids have no idea what they mean).

I tried not to appear too excited… but I was.

I liked being around Carly.

She looked at me while Mum and Penny made suggestions on dates and times and rolled her eyes.

But then she smiled and her eyes lit up and I decided that I was REALLY going to enjoy my new school.

Mum asked me what I was smiling about on the way home in the car and I replied, "Oh, nothing."

But, to be honest, I hadn't known that I was smiling.

That night, when I was heading from the bathroom to my bedroom, I heard Carly's name mentioned by Mum, talking to Dad. I couldn't hear what his reply was, but there was an upward lilt on the end of his sentence and they both chuckled afterwards.

I can't be sure, but I think I was still smiling when I fell asleep.

TWENTY-THREE

The next day was Friday, but I didn't get chance to speak to Archie, as he wasn't at school.

Isabella-Banana got into a bit of a fight with another girl in the class at lunchtime. I'm not sure what started it, but I saw the other girl, Heidi, actually slap Isabella-Banana. This was in the dinner hall and none of the dinner ladies saw it, but they did hear it and Miss Whittell was looking when Isabella-Banana retaliated by grabbing Heidi by the hair (which must have been difficult because she's smaller than Heidi) and launching a kick at her shins. Miss Whittell waded in then and grabbed both of them – she's a big woman – escorting them straight out of the dinner hall.

It caused quite a stir, I can tell you!

Everyone was talking about it, even the people who weren't actually there.

For example, Jack (he of the big eyes) had been sat next to me eating his lunch, then had finished and gone outside with his mate, Ethan. So he hadn't seen anything at all, but I heard him later in class, explaining it blow by blow to Harry. "… And then she picked up her lunch plate and literally *threw* it at Heidi's head!"

Harry was sat there, open-mouthed lapping it all up.

Desperate!

Stooge 2 of the short skirt and pink knickers had stood up straight afterwards and followed Miss Whittell out of the dinner hall, but was marched right back in two minutes later.

We all sat there, too stunned to finish our lunches. Neither girl returned and it was fifteen minutes into the afternoon before the headteacher brought them both back to class. She asked Mr Antinori for a quiet word first, so he left us alone in the classroom while they went outside to talk.

Jess and Pink Knickers were shushing everyone, desperate to hear what was being said outside.

It was murmuring at first, but then Mr Antinori started shouting.

I'd never heard him shout before. I mean, he'd raised his voice a few times, but WOW – this was like a nuclear bomb. I couldn't help it; I was scared.

I didn't catch everything he said, but he definitely said, "… ABSOLUTELY DISGUSTED WITH THE PAIR OF YOU!"

We were all turned round, facing the door, but as soon as the handle started to move, as one, the whole class whipped back around and faced their desks, not daring to look up.

I did hear some whimpering, from – I assume – Heidi and when I caught a look at Isabella-Banana shortly afterwards, her face was red and blotchy from crying.

Exciting times!

Mr Antinori was very tense for the rest of the afternoon and didn't smile at all. It was a depressing end to what had been a great week to that point.

When the final bell went, he took both Heidi and Isabella-Banana outside to their parents. Most of the class rushed after them to try and watch, but I felt a bit sorry for them all, so I lagged behind, not in any great hurry to get out, as I was meeting Dad that night and he was usually a bit later than mum.

As I was grabbing my PE kit off my peg, Carly appeared next to me.

"Well," she began, "that was certainly an 'atmospheric' afternoon, wasn't it?"

I laughed, happy to let some of the tension out.

"Yes, it was. I've never heard Mr Antinori shout like that before. Does it happen a lot?"

She smiled, all green eyes and a few freckles on her nose. "No, don't worry. I think you'll find nobody will do anything bad for a while now, after hearing that."

"Thank goodness!"

We both walked to the classroom door together, not talking, but comfortable with each other's company.

Just before we got there, the door flung open and Mr Antinori walked in with a look of thunder on his face. A moment later, he saw us both in front of him and I think he must have realised we were startled because his expression changed immediately.

"Oh! Hey guys, sorry. I thought you'd all left."

We were both a bit flustered and ended up looking at each other and then him.

"Erm…" I managed.

"Sorry," spluttered Carly.

I think we both felt like we were in trouble, but I don't know what for.

Thankfully, he rescued us.

"No, no. It's me who should be sorry. I've just come from speaking to parents and I didn't think there'd be anyone here. Are you both as happy that it's the weekend as I am?"

Carly did what Carly does and smiled at him, which made him smile in return.

What an amazing gift the girl has! I know, I know, I'm ridiculous.

"Are you seeing your gran this weekend, Oscar?" he asked me.

"I'm not sure," I replied. "I think she's on a trip with her next-door neighbour."

He raised an eyebrow. "Well I want to thank you once again, Oscar. I'm going to see my gran again tomorrow, I'm taking my little girl with me and we're calling at the bakery on the way, to pick up a cake."

"How old is your little girl, Mr Antinori?" asked Carly.

"Oh, she's only two, bless her and I don't think she really likes seeing her great-gran. I think she finds it a bit scary, but it really has an effect on the old lady, I can tell you."

He looked a bit upset at this point and I tried to quickly come up with something to cheer him up, so I blurted out the first thing that came to mind.

"You should bring her into school," I said.

They both looked at me, like I'd gone mad, but then Mr Antinori's face changed and he looked out of the window, like he was thinking. So I carried on – I thought, well, I've gone this far...

"In my old school, we wrote letters to our dads and invited them in for a day. 'Men Behaving Dadly' we called it. It was really good fun. Maybe we could do something like that? Have a gran day?"

Carly was nodding her head now. "That would be ace, Oscar. My gran would LOVE that!"

Mr Antinori looked at me, both (bushy) eyebrows meeting in the middle as he looked down at me, with his hands on his hips. "Oscar, I think that is one of the best ideas I've ever heard. I'm going to give it some thought this weekend, how we could make it work. Thank you."

I shrugged my shoulders, "No worries, Mr Antinori." And I started heading for the door, with Carly right behind me.

"Have a great weekend, both of you," he called after us.

TWENTY-FOUR

I was talking to Alex outside school on Monday, when I noticed Archie arriving. He arrived alone and I began to wonder whether he had any close friends – I'd never actually seen him with anyone.

I waited for a polite gap in the conversation with Alex and walked over to where Archie stood, alone, watching a group of girls by the door.
"Hi, Archie, are you feeling better?" I asked him.

This was the first time that I'd ever said a word to him before and he turned to look at me with a look that said exactly that. Like, why are *you* talking to *me*? He tilted his head on one side; like you see dogs do and began to look uncomfortable.
It was hard to read what was going on.
He didn't walk away and he didn't tell me to go away, but he didn't smile and, incredibly – he didn't actually speak back to me.
At all.

My question (from like two minutes before) was hanging in the air between us.
Should I be following it up? If I walked away now, would I look rude? Stupid? Both?
For the moment I continued to stand there, looking at him, but not looking at him, my eyes kind of darting about, occasionally daring to go back to his eyes.

Then, all of a sudden, he spoke.
"I'm… fine," he managed.
It had taken him almost four minutes to reply. Very strange from the boy with lightning sharp wit in the classroom!

I decided to plough on.

"Well, I don't know if anyone told you, but you missed a very interesting Friday."

He went back to looking at me.

He had a very dark eye colour. I couldn't actually tell you what colour they were – so dark, they were almost black.

Almost lifeless.

Quite frightening.

"Oh yeah? Why?"

Two-minute response time – it was getting better.

"There was a fight at lunchtime! In the dinner hall."

He looked at me and there was a flicker momentarily in his dark eyes. Had I interested him?

"Who?"

Again, I wondered at the difference between this Archie, who was trying so hard not to communicate, like he was saving his words, and the boy who seemed to come alive and enjoy the humour in his outbursts in class.

"Isabella-Banana and Heidi." I'd said it before I realised, in my eagerness to draw Archie out.

His expression changed now, a smile creeping onto his face, his cheeks rising and his eyes coming to life.

"Isabella-Banana?" he replied.

"Isabella-Banana," he repeated.

His smile got wider as he appeared to be thinking about this. Then he nodded.

"Isabella-Banana," he said for a third time. "...That's brilliant. Well funny!"

Then the bell went and Archie picked up his bag. Had I made a friend here? Were we now friends? It was so hard to tell. He *had* laughed, or at least smiled.

Archie had started towards the door, but then he stopped and looked at me.

"Come on then," he said.

And that was it.

I *think* it was then that I became Archie's friend.

But I wasn't sure.

TWENTY-FIVE

Registration was 'interesting' – the format was the same as normal, with Mr Antinori calling out our first names and us replying.

"Jess."

"Here."

"Oscar."

"Here."

Etc.

You get the idea.

All going well until we got to, "Isabella-…"

And before Mr Antinori could get the word, "Jane" out, Archie had jumped in, coughing the word, "BANANA!" into his hand.

Mr Antinori looked up from his screen.

I turned around to look at Archie and saw Isabella looking across at him with one eyebrow raised, wondering if this was something that she needed to challenge.

Archie was just looking round the room, seemingly bored, as if nothing had happened, other than him clearing his throat.

Nobody else in the class seemed to be remotely interested; they hadn't noticed anything, by the look of it.

I turned back around to Mr Antinori, who was still looking at Archie, suspiciously.

"Are you quite OK, Mr Kershaw?" he asked him.

"Yes thanks, Mr Antinori. I've just got a bit of a cough. My mum says I need to get some phlegm up."

Mr Antinori didn't appear to be completely convinced, but he carried on anyway.

As I passed Archie, on my way to my English place, he looked up at me, mouthing, 'banana,' as he carried on to his seat, devious smile on his face.

"Banana?" Carly said. "Why 'banana'?"

We were sat, facing each other in the dinner hall. Other kids had already eaten and left, so it was just the two of us at that end of the table.

I finished the last of my sandwich (corned beef and brown sauce, in case you are interested) and smiled, "Why not?"

"But it makes absolutely no sense. Jane sounds nothing like banana. I don't get it." She certainly looked puzzled. I tried to explain further.

"You see, that's the whole point. If I called her 'Isabella-Train', or 'Isabella-Brain' it just isn't funny, because it's too similar."

She raised her shoulders and shook her head.

"Besides," I continued. "The word 'banana' is amusing; it's completely out of context and unexpected."

"Maybe it's a boy thing?" she said, zipping up her lunch bag.

"Maybe."

At that exact moment, Archie sat down next to us.

"Banana!" he said, with a goofy grin on his face, as if he was saying hello.

"She doesn't get it," I replied, nodding towards Carly, who had her eyes raised skywards, shaking her head again.

"I'm going outside," she announced, standing up.

I wondered if she wanted me to go with her. It was difficult to say, so I erred on the side of caution.

"I'm going to stay here and discuss fruit humour with Mr Kershaw," I responded.

"OK, see ya."

And she was off, without looking back.

Archie was already tucking into his lunch, which seemed to be entirely composed of whole pieces of fruit and vegetables. At that moment, he was eating – I kid you not – a green pepper, like it was an apple.

I stared at him for a moment, then he looked at me and smiled, "What?"

"What *are* you eating, Archie?"

He waved it at me, "What does it look like? It's a green pepper."

"But why?"

He took another CRUNCH, by way of response. I'll give it to him: it sounded fresh.

"Don't you ever eat, I dunno, sandwiches?"

He was nibbling around the stalk at the top now and stopped. "Nah! Boring." And he went back to his pepper.

"Does your mum make your lunch?" I asked.

He stopped again and looked at me, "Make?" he answered. "How's she going to *make* a pepper? Don't be daft – I get them out of the fridge."

A good point, but it wasn't what I was getting at. Clearly this was normal for Archie and who am I to say what 'normal' means? Just because everyone else brings a sandwich, it doesn't mean that they are right and Archie is wrong.

"Do you eat these every day?" I pointed at the contents of his lunchbox.

He was popping cherries in his mouth now.

"No. It depends what's in the fridge. Sometimes I bring celery, or carrots. Last week I brought a cauliflower."

WOW!

I don't think I really *enjoy* cauliflower when it's smothered with cheese sauce and dipped in gravy.

On its own? Yeeuch!

I was just about to tell him this, when he asked me, "So, is she your girlfriend then?"

Blimey.

I decided to stall, while I thought about it.

"Who?"

"Who? Carly, you idiot! You didn't think I was talking about Isabella-Banana, did you?" he replied, with a lot of stress on the word 'banana'.

I laughed.

Still thinking.

What was the right answer here? She *wasn't* my girlfriend, was she?

"Nah!" I told him, "We're just friends. My mum's friends with her auntie."

Like that mattered, but it seemed to put him off the idea.

"What about you? Do you have a girlfriend?" I asked him.

"Me?" He dropped a strawberry on the table. "Don't be crazy! Who would I fancy in our class?"

"Well, you do like fruit," I pointed out. "Maybe '*bananas*' are what you have a passion for?"

Archie looked up at me again, then suddenly burst out laughing. A really LOUD laughter, coming right from his belly. It wasn't even one of those laughs that makes you want to laugh. In fact, I was a bit embarrassed. It was too loud; people were staring at us!

But then I looked at Archie. He was really having fun and I'd helped him do that. Everything Carly had told me about him and his dad and how he'd had a bad year last year came back to me.

I felt good.

I think I'd found a friend.

TWENTY-SIX

There was no cough in the afternoon register, but I did turn around and catch Archie's eye, when Mr Antinori said, "Isabella-Jane.' Archie was smiling back at me, like we were both part of a conspiracy.

As I was turning back to face the front, I noticed Carly staring at me from her place. When our eyes met, she just shook her head and rolled her eyes.

Monday afternoon was PE and we were doing tennis. When we got out onto the court, Mr Antinori made us all do a warm up, which consisted of running around the outside of the playground, while he set stuff up.

Then he mixed us all up and assigned us partners.

My first partner was Pink Knickers, which made me smile when he called it out (her real name, you'll be interested to know, is Daisy; she doesn't look much like a Daisy), but she refused to look at me... which made me smile more.

We had to play together against another pair.

Mr Antinori had already taught us how to serve. When I say 'taught', I mean he'd *showed* us how to serve; now we had to try to put it into action. We had a net – of sorts – that unrolled and stood on small, plastic legs. The other team (Yusuf and Jess) served first. Yusuf managed to get most of the serves over the net, but even he smiled when he didn't. I got one of his serves back too, but it wasn't in the court. I think Yusuf must have played before; he seemed quite comfortable with it. Jess didn't seem at all interested – she kept spinning her racket around and didn't even attempt to go for the ball when Daisy Pink Knickers hit it towards her.

Daisy was pretty good too, even if she was completely ignoring me. I wondered if Mr Antinori had put us together on purpose, to try and encourage us to get on with each other.

It wasn't working.

And it was about to get worse.

After the third game – we were only to play four, each serving once – it was my turn to serve.

Now, I had played tennis a bit and I do have decent co-ordination, so I was quite excited. Even though Yusuf had won his serve, Daisy had served well to win that game and we had easily beaten Jess's serve, so we were 2-1 up, with one game to play.

My first serve was in and Jess didn't even *try* to return it. Then I served a double fault against Yusuf – I think I was worried that he'd hit it straight back at me. I beat Jess again, then on the next serve, even though Yusuf got it back, Daisy hit a fantastic volley to win the point.

"Nice shot, Daisy!" I shouted, but she didn't even look at me.

Hey, at least *I* was trying.

So, it was 40-15 and I was serving for the game.

Now, as I said, Jess was not interested, so it seemed like we had it sewn up, but I served my first into the net and, being careful to make sure my second serve at least cleared the net, I hit a safe lob over the net to Jess's side.

"Go on, Jess," called Yusuf. "You can hit that!"

And, amazingly, she did.

Her shot cleared the net and somehow landed almost exactly halfway between Daisy and me. I was already running for the ball, thinking about hitting the winning volley, when I realised that Daisy was doing the same thing.

It was too late to pull out and we both ended up running into each other.

Now… to be fair to me, I did actually get my racket to the ball AND if we are thinking purely about the aim of this activity, the ball did go over the net and past Jess, to win the point *and therefore* the game.

But…

When I turned around to celebrate with my partner and make sure that she was OK, as we had collided with each other, imagine my surprise to find her lying on the floor, with her legs akimbo, showing me that today, Monday, was obviously orange knicker day.

You know when something is in front of you that you know you are not supposed to look at? Like when someone has a large mole on their face, or a birthmark, or something like that?

Well, that was me.

Frozen.

Arm in the air in celebration.

Shouting, "YEEEESSSS!"

While staring at Daisy's orange knickers.

On this occasion nobody else saw this. Yusuf and Jess were both in discussion, Yusuf no longer smiling, but giving his partner some lessons on concentration during a game and the other kids were all engrossed in their games.

So this was just a private moment, between me, Daisy and her underwear.

She didn't cry this time either, which was good.

She just stood up, straightened her skirt… and hit me with the racket.

TWENTY-SEVEN

As the week went on, I started spending more and more time with Archie. He was actually a really fun guy to be with and I didn't understand why he'd been such a loner. I wondered if it was because he'd distanced himself from everyone last year and so all the other boys had simply become good mates, so it had become hard for him to get back in with the friendships?

Well, it seemed to be my gain, so I wasn't going to worry about it.

Mr Antinori hadn't yet mentioned my idea of inviting grandparents in, so I guessed he'd dismissed the idea.

Carly and I were getting on well and the lunch date seemed to be have been set up for Saturday.

Now, when I say 'date' that was what my mum had taken to calling it. Whether Carly considered it a date, or whether mum and Penny actually had ulterior motives and were trying to set us up, or whether it was just me that was worrying about nothing, I don't know, but I was spending a lot of time thinking about it.

What should I wear?

Now, don't get me wrong, I've not got a large wardrobe of clothes to choose from, but I do have a couple of outfits that could be considered 'smart', that Mum and Dad referred to, if we were going somewhere that meant that I'd have to look 'smart'.

So, if I put something like this on, would Mum wonder if something was up? Because, to be honest, whenever we are going out and she says, "Oscar, put something smart on!" I generally reply, "Oh Mum, do I *have* to?"

So, you can see, if I put something smart on without having to be prompted, then that's just a giveaway, isn't it?

Or, do I play it cool and just wear something casual?

But then what if Carly dresses up and I look like I've just 'come off the building site', as Dad likes to say?

It's quite a problem.

Carly did mention the lunch a few times during the week and she didn't seem to be embarrassed, or uncomfortable about it, so I behaved the same back with her (still using Dad's strategy). Apparently, we were going to a coffee shop in town and *everybody* raves about this place. I'd never heard anybody mention it before and couldn't even remember what it was called, but Carly was incredibly excited about going there.

She didn't even seem to mind that Archie knew about the 'lunch date'. I'd kept quiet about the whole thing during school, in case I upset anyone by saying the wrong thing, but then Carly brought it up at lunchtime, while Archie was gnawing away on a stick of celery.

"Archie, have you been to that new coffee shop in town?" (She might have said the name here, but I couldn't remember it.)

Archie just looked at her, doing his head tilt thing, raising one brow, while lowering the other – which I'd learnt meant 'are you insane?'

Anyway, she'd then gone on to tell him that we were both going on Saturday for lunch, clearly very proud of the whole thing.

I think – maybe – she was proud of the fact that she was going to the coffee shop, not that she was going there with me, but one never knows…

Archie never brought it up with me afterwards. No 'ooh, you're going on a date with Carly', or anything like that. It all just appeared to be accepted.

Which just made me a bit more nervous, to be honest.

So, Friday, leaving school, Archie and I were walking together, when he suddenly began to tell me about his mum having a boyfriend.

He just blurted it out.

It was clearly on his mind and I wondered how long he'd been worrying about it.

It was Dad's night to pick me up, so I knew there was no rush to get away.

"He's a Man United fan – can you believe that?"

"Oh dear, I'm sorry, Archie. That's awful," I sympathised.

"I know. So, he's coming round tonight. I've not actually met him yet."

I didn't have any experience in this area at all. What advice do you give when you've not been in this position? Was Archie just sharing the news? Did he just need to say this out loud, to make sense of it all for himself, or was he looking to me for some wise words?

Did I have any wise words?

Fortunately, he carried on talking, "He's bringing his daughter – who is about my age apparently – and he's also bringing a curry, because Mum's told him I love curry. Then we're watching a film."

This was my moment, "What are you watching?"

"Something old, it's about some guy who skives off school and does lots of mad stuff in a Ferrari."

"*Ferris Bueller's Day Off*!" I said. "You'll love that film, Archie. It's really fantastic!"

He looked brighter, so I thought I'd continue.

"You know, he might actually be quite cool, if he's bringing a curry and a good film."

And, just like that, his mood changed.

He stopped walking and his eyes actually darkened.

"Yeah well, he's not my dad, so I don't want him thinking he is."

Oops!

I'd obviously said the wrong thing.

I could have backed off here, but I decided this was what friends were supposed to do, they were supposed to be honest with each other. There's no point ignoring what's happening, you might as well face things.

Archie looked like he'd shut down, and retreated into himself, like he was before we became friends and that first morning, when responses were difficult to get out of him.

"Maybe he's not trying to be your dad, Archie. Maybe he's just trying to get to know you by doing something nice?"

He still looked unhappy.

I tried something else.

"If your mum likes him enough to want you to meet him, then it's got to be worth giving him a chance, I reckon."

We were stood just outside the school gates and people were having to walk around us. Nobody actually said anything, but I could see that some people were annoyed. A woman with a pram was approaching and we were in the way.

I tried to get Archie to move, by pointing her out and walking to one side, but when I turned around, he had just stood his ground and was staring into space.

The woman said, "Excuse me, love."

But Archie just ignored her.

"Archie, you're in the way," I said, in as nice a way as I could manage.

He just looked at me.

"You don't know my mum. You haven't met her!" he delivered in a flat tone, but with enough feeling to make me clear about how it was meant to be taken. 'You have no idea how we are dealing with things,' was what he was saying.

I know I hadn't been friends with Archie for long, but I'd started talking with him for the right reasons and we'd become friends by accident, without trying. Once again, I didn't think I had any reason to feel guilty.

Again, I was starting to wonder if the rest of my life was going to be about feeling guilty for one thing after another.

It didn't seem fair.

They didn't teach you about that in school.

The woman had given up waiting for Archie to move by now and was pushing her pram around the new statue of the sulking child, whilst tutting loudly and making comments about manners.

I couldn't really blame her, but what could I do?

A big girl from Year 4, who I'd seen playing football on the playground, then came up to Archie and pushed him.

He lost his balance for a moment, but recovered and tried to throw an arm in her direction. The arm missed, but it was clear what he was aiming for and another parent, someone's dad, came over.

"Oi, what do you think you're doing, lad?"

Again, Archie chose to ignore him, refusing to even look in his direction.

I decided I had to step in and try again.

"Sorry, mister," I said, putting an arm around Archie and looking at the dad, who seemed like he didn't really know what to do, now he was here. "My mate's a bit upset, that's all. He's had some bad news."

The dad stepped back a little, nodding, like he had done the job he'd come to do. He straightened his t-shirt, which wasn't untidy in the first place, but it was one of those little habits that we all have to help us in different situations (like me saying 'anyway').

"Right, OK then. He just needs to calm down that's all. He can't be trying to hit people," he said, recovering his authority.

"To be fair to Archie, he was pushed first," I replied, sticking up for my mate.

"Yeah, but she's a girl. You don't go around hitting girls."

He was pointing now, but he was moving away and eventually he turned around, looking for (I suppose) his child.

There seemed to be no sense in arguing further. I wouldn't win.

I turned back to Archie, who was looking at me. I couldn't read his expression, but he seemed to have softened.

"What was my bad news?" he croaked.

"Pardon?"

At least he was communicating. But what was he talking about?

"You told that man I'd had some bad news. What was it?"

I needed to be careful here. I sensed the answer to this question was going to shape our future friendship. He was pretty close to either standing here, outside school all weekend, or running off home.

"Oh right, yes," I began. "That's right. Your mum's boyfriend is a Man United fan. I mean, how much worse could it get?"

The corner of his mouth began to turn up.

I smiled and shrugged my shoulders.

There was a BEEP behind me. I looked and saw Dad pulling up to the kerbside.

I turned back to Archie, who was smiling now.

"Oscar," Dad called over.

I waved an arm in his direction, to show I'd heard him.

"Why don't you come and meet my dad?" I said to Archie.

"Yeah, sure," he replied and followed me over to the car.

Dad had reached across and opened the passenger door from the inside. I leaned in, as he was moving his bag off the seat and putting it into the back.

"Hi, Dad, this is my friend, Archie."

Dad leaned forward and down a bit, so he could see Archie clearly.

"Hi, Archie, how's it going?"

"Good thanks," he replied.

We'd very quickly reached that point where everyone had stopped talking and nobody knew what to say, luckily Dad jumped in.

"Why don't we arrange it so that Archie can come over to ours sometime?" he said, looking at me.

I looked at Archie, lifting my eyebrows questioningly.

"Yeah," he said. "Sounds great."

"Right then," said Dad. "We'll get Oscar's mum to give your mum a bell and set something up."

"Great! Thanks, Dad."

"Right then, get in, son, we've got to call at the Co-op on the way home. See you soon, Archie."

"See ya."

And with that, Archie was off home.

TWENTY-EIGHT – The Lunch 'Date'

I only got changed three times.

Well, between you and me, it was four, but there were only three possible outfits.

In the end, I went with some 'smart' black jeans and a long-sleeved t-shirt, which said 'California' on it. I'd never been to California, but I didn't think that mattered. I often looked around at people's shirts, with names of places and numbers on them and wondered if the people wearing them had actually ever been to those places. It's a pretty good idea for money-making really – just buy a load of plain t-shirts, grab a map of the world, stick a pin in it and use that place name alongside a random 2-digit number. Or a date? Years seem quite popular. Get it printed on the t-shirts in a crazy font and sell them for 50% profit.

Try it.

You might be surprised.

If you make a lot of money though, remember me.

Anyway, I washed my face (yes, I know!) and wrestled with my hair, so that it didn't look neat, but it wasn't scruffy.

Dad had left some of that spray-on deodorant on the side in the bathroom, the type that is on all the adverts on TV, where girls find the wearer irresistible. Surely Mum had seen those ads? Was Dad secretly thinking about being irresistible when he put it on?

It's interesting how you think about adverts when you use the products. Isn't it supposed to work the other way around? Anyway, I'll hold my hand up; I *was* wondering whether Carly would find me irresistible when I showed up smelling like the blokes on the adverts. It was a strange smell, more like chemicals than anything else, but what do I know?

I went downstairs and did that thing where you know that both parents are looking at you because you've tried that extra bit harder today, but you avoid eye contact and pretend you haven't noticed and that, as far as you are concerned, you've done nothing out of the ordinary.

I could literally feel the weight of their stares as they were WILLING me to meet their eyes. It was like that scene in the first Star Wars – which is actually part four, but that's a whole other story – when Obi-Wan tells Han Solo that the Millennium Falcon is being pulled into the Death Star by their tractor beam. Mum and Dad's tractor beam was pulling my eyes towards theirs, but I was the young apprentice Jedi, standing in his parents' kitchen, fighting against the forces of evil.

Or something.

I walked over to the cupboard and got a bowl out, concentrating on my new 'Jedi' skills and doing really well until dad cheated and tried to make me laugh.

"Ooh, Kate," he started, in a breathy, deep voice. "What's that *lovely* smell? It smells like... teen spirit, except cleaner."

We all cracked up then.

I tried to resist, but it was pointless. They were laughing, so I might as well laugh along with them.

"You look lovely, son," beamed Mum.

What do you say? I just mumbled a "Thanks."

"So, what time is the BIG DATE then?" asked Dad.

I just glared at him.

"Anthony!" Mum snapped at Dad. "Leave him alone."

Mum hardly-ever called Dad by his first name, and certainly not Anthony – he was Tony to his friends and I'd only ever heard Anthony when his mum, my gran, spoke to him.

He looked a bit wounded by Mum's attack – which served him right, but I still felt sorry for him. I mean, I'd been on the wrong end of a few people shouting at me over the past few weeks.

"It's OK, Mum," I said to her. Then, to Dad, "We're meeting them at twelve, at some ultra-hip coffee shop in town."

Dad winked at me.

"Well, I think you are really brave, Oscar," he said. "Going out with three women. Do you need back-up?"

Mum punched him, playfully on the shoulder, making him drop the newspaper he was reading.

"He'll be absolutely fine, thank you!" she told him. "And besides, it's not a *big date*, it's just friends getting together for some lunch and a chat."

I know that Mum said that to make me relax, but I couldn't help feeling a bit disappointed. I think I'd convinced myself that it was a date and I'd revved myself up for it a bit.

Who was I kidding?

I WAS TEN!

My face must have registered my thoughts, because Dad jumped back in, "Well, I think that this, what's she called? Carly? She'd be crazy not to want to be Oscar's girlfriend and when he shows up looking cool and smelling like a god, then it's game over!"

He winked at me again.

Mum rolled her eyes.

I tried to be cool again and keep a straight face – but failed.

TWENTY-NINE – The Lunch 'Date', Part Two

We parked up by the church in the middle of town and Mum went to get a parking ticket.

She came back, telling me that we had two hours and asking whether was that long enough?

"Erm, I don't know," I replied.

Was she *really* asking me, or was this another example of someone talking out loud and hoping to get an answer from themselves? I was starting to notice this a lot recently.

So many repeated themes in my Year 6 life!

The coffee shop was called Café Olé and, on the display outside above the windows, it had a design of a matador pulling back a big cape to reveal a cup of, what could only be, coffee. As we approached, we saw Penny and Carly in the window waving frantically to attract our attention.

Inside it was pretty cool, all done in Spanish colours of red and yellow, with shiny black everywhere. Carly and Penny seemed to have grabbed the best table, a kind of booth in the window, looking out at the main shopping street, giving us a great view of the town, but also giving passers-by a view of us, looking cool, in the window of the coolest place in town. All of a sudden, I realised why everyone raved about this place.

Penny jumped up and told me to get in her place, which suited me, as 1) it was right next to the window, and 2) more importantly, I was right opposite Carly, who – I might add – looked great!

Obviously having an aunt who was a hairdresser helped. I couldn't possibly explain what style her hair was in, as I'm a boy, but it was so shiny and clean that it almost sparkled. Even Mum made a comment about her beautiful hair.

Penny looked like she'd just got out of the toaster, as usual, then added a blond wig and makeup.

"What do you want to drink, love?" Mum asked me.

I tried to be stylish. I only really knew a couple of drinks from the occasional Starbucks visit in the US, so I tried one of those. "Can I have a caramel macchiato?" I asked her.

"I'm not sure they'll have those, Oscar, but I'll see what I can do." Then she asked Penny, "Are we having something to eat?"

"Ooh yes," Penny replied, in an over-excited voice. "I'll come with you, Kate, then these two can '*catch up*'."

She said the last two words with a whole lot of emphasis and left us with a big smile of overwhite teeth.

Embarrassing!

"Does your auntie know how brown she is?" I asked.

"I know!" Carly replied. "It's crazy!"

I think we were both happy that I'd changed the subject.
"I had a teacher last year, who told us that sunbathing was incredibly bad and that our grandkids will…" Then I stopped, having realised what I'd just said and made things worse. "… not that *WE* will be having grandkids."

From a great start thirty seconds ago, Carly was now looking at me in horror.

"I didn't mean *OUR* grandkids, you know, yours and mine together…"

I knew I was making it worse, but I couldn't seem to stop, "… I just meant that, you know, other people's grandkids…"

I stopped again; Carly was doing that laugh thing.

She had her eyes closed and was doing that sing-song laugh and it just diffused the tension, like it did before.

Amazing.

I glanced out of the window at the people in the street and wondered if any of them were as happy as I was at that moment.

And then, I saw her...
Isabella-Banana.
And she was upset and shouting at someone.
"Carly, look!"

THIRTY (The Aside – Tony Delta)

Tony Delta, christened (people used to be christened) Anthony Michael Delta – his parents didn't have the same 'quirky' humour – was born in the 1960s. He wears this like a badge of honour and mentions it a lot. I'm not quite sure what was *cool* about the 1960s, but it makes him happy; apparently that's when music really began. The surname 'Delta' is unusual and it comes from his grandfather, who was from North Africa.

This is actually a pretty interesting story: after the first World War ended, with lots of people dead and not many left to run the factories and do all the manual labour, some of the remaining troops put up trestle tables and chairs in North Africa (I'm pretty sure this part is slightly made up) and encouraged single men to 'Come to Europe – the land of opportunity'.

My great-granddad was one of those men, who shuffled over to the table, interested in what the men in uniform were selling.

Before he knew it, he'd signed up and they were shipping him to Turin, (or Torino, as Dad's side of the family insist on calling it) Italy, to work in a factory, making Fiat cars.

Eventually he met my great-grandma, Mabel, who was a nurse, originally from Halifax. They had a whirlwind romance (again, I think the story is embellished here) and got married, living in a little flat, with a balcony that overlooked some football field. Mabel got pregnant, as people tend to do when they have a balcony overlooking a football field (not really – I made that up) and made the life-changing decision to move back to Yorkshire, so that Mabel's mum and younger sister could help with the child-care.

So, at this stage, my great grandfather had really lived a very interesting life, but the most interesting part was his name. The story goes that the soldier, who took his details down on the trestle table either couldn't – or didn't want to – understand the name of the young, slightly dark-skinned man in front of him, so he made it up, as he had been doing all morning and, because he was putting him into the fourth pile – to go to the industrial north of Italy – he chose Delta – again with the phonetic alphabet.

Delta worked quite well in Italy and he probably fit in better than he would have done with a Libyan name, so it all worked out well.

Fast forward to today and my dad, Antonio Michele (as he insists he is really called after a bottle of chianti) Delta is a manager of a shipping company – owned by Isabella-Banana's dad – which deals primarily with Italy. He speaks fluent Italian and tans well, but not on a par with Penny.

I don't know much about his boss, other than he's called John Rawes and does, or doesn't wear pink knickers, depending on who you talk to.

But I was guessing that it was his boss that we were now looking at – the angry, red-faced man, who had hold of Isabella-Banana's arm in the middle of town on a Saturday afternoon, while she was screaming at him.

THIRTY-ONE (Back to the lunch date)

"O... M... G!" Carly was transfixed, staring through the window, as, I noticed, were the couple at the table behind her, the lady pointing, finger pressed up against the glass window.

The man, who we were presuming was her dad, was quite smartly dressed: dark blue jeans, white shirt tucked into them – is that allowed? He also had a dark blue blazer on, with gold buttons that were flashing in the sunlight, as he wrestled with his daughter. He seemed to be trying to restrain Isabella-Banana, which just looked wrong, given her age and he was drawing quite a crowd of people, who had all stopped to watch.

Isabella-Banana wasn't crying, she just looked very, VERY angry and was clearly shouting at him now.

One lady from the onlookers seemed to be trying to intervene by talking to him and had drawn his attention, as he had stopped grabbing at his daughter and was turning to face her.

"What on earth is going on out there?" asked Penny as she started putting cups and plates onto the table.

There really did seem to be about fifty people stood around now and it was obvious that Mr Rawes had taken stock of the situation and looked noticeably calmer, as if he was putting a different face on.

"That," began Carly, turning to her auntie, who was leaning on the table staring out of the window, "is Isabella-Jane from our class, but I've no idea who the man is."

"Oh, that's her dad," I said, nonchalantly.

"REALLY?" they both said turning to me. And it occurred to me that, maybe he wasn't. Maybe it was a random stranger and I was doing her dad a huge disservice, but it didn't seem likely, so I carried on, convinced.

"Yeah," I continued. "He's my dad's boss." "Who's Dad's boss?" asked Mum, finally arriving, late to the party.

"That bloke out there," I said pointing out of the window.

And that…
    Was when Isabella-Banana decided to turn round and looked straight in our direction, to see me pointing directly at her.
    "Oh dear," said Carly. "She doesn't look happy."

"What, the man in the blue blazer with the big gold watch?" asked Penny.
    "He's your dad's boss?" asked Mum.

So everyone was now waiting for an answer from me and I belatedly lowered my pointing finger, to see Isabella-Banana walking towards the coffee shop.
    "This really can't be good," Carly offered, looking at me in horror.

I looked back out of the window, to see that a couple of police officers had now turned up and were talking to Mr Rawes, who was offering his palms up to them, as if to say there was nothing to worry about.

But there was.

Because the coffee shop door had now opened and my nemesis was walking towards our table.

"Any suggestions?" I asked, looking at my three companions, who simply stared back at me with open mouths.

THIRTY-TWO (curiouser and curiouser)

Carly was right; she didn't look happy.

In fact, she looked like she was holding back tears.

As Isabella-Banana walked through the coffee shop, all eyes followed her, some people actually turning in their seats to get a better view.

She was dressed in jeans way trendier than mine: black, skinny, with rips at the knees and was wearing a Nirvana t-shirt, the one with the baby in the swimming pool. Even dressed down, she still looked like the posh girl that she was and now she was about to tell me I shouldn't be staring at her (and maybe pointing at her) in front of my mum and two other people.

Was I going to stand for it?

Well, I didn't last time, did I? I knew that my sarcasm was going to be needed, but strangely found myself worried for her – hadn't she been through enough in the last ten minutes?

Also, did I really want to cause more problems for my dad? It was his boss out there, being interviewed by police, after all. I know that they'd caused it all, but it wasn't looking like a particularly good day for the Rawes family, was it?

She was almost at the table now and I realised that I was just going to have to respond to whatever happened.

Mum and Penny were both smiling sympathetically at her, mum clutching her coffee for defence. I took a deep breath as she stopped at the head of the table.

"Hi, Oscar, hi, Carly," she said, by way of greeting. "Is it OK if I join you?"

I don't think I could have been more shocked.

I looked at Carly, who was looking back at me with an expression that can only have mirrored mine.

Firstly, Isabella-Banana had never, ever said, "Hi," to me, she had certainly never greeted me at all, but it was her tone... almost... pleading?

I looked back at her, looking in her eyes and it was clear how close she was to breaking. At that moment, we were her only friends, her last chance, almost – that's how it felt. I was just about to reply, when I realised that Mum and Penny were already ahead of me.

"Of course. Sit down here," said Penny, dragging a chair from another table and motioning that she should take her seat, next to Carly.

"Let me get you a drink, love," Mum was saying. "Would you like a coffee? Or a juice?"

Isabella-Banana was looking relieved, as she got sat in her seat, visibly relaxing and it seemed that the additional interest from around us was setting down, as normality was taking over.

"Erm, could I have a cappuccino, please?" she asked, in a small voice.

"Of course you can. You just sit there and Penny and I will leave you to catch up a bit."

And with that, there were three of us: Isabella-Banana staring down at her lap and Carly and I looking back and forth between her and each other, both desperately willing the other to open the awkward conversation, which somehow had to begin.

Thankfully, Carly grasped the nettle.

"Are you OK?"

Slowly, she lifted her face, tears running down her cheeks. I quickly grabbed at a handful of napkins from the table and thrust them towards her.

"Oh, thanks," she said and tried to smile at me. "I bet I look a right mess, don't I?"

I was hoping that Carly was going to step in here and tell her, 'No, don't worry, you look fine.'

But she didn't and honesty is the best policy, so I jumped in with both feet.

"Well…" is what I came out with, letting it dangle.

"Oscar!" Carly barked at me, with her mouth wide open.

But it had the desired effect, as Isabella-Banana seemed to be laughing quietly – at the same time as crying.

Bizarrely, I wondered whether there was a human version of a rainbow? Someone laughing and crying at the same time MUST be similar in reaction to it raining and being sunny? I resolved to revisit this and returned to the scene in front of me.

"Don't worry," I told her. "I've made far more of a fool of myself since I started at Netherlea. I've realised that people quickly forget and you've just got to get on with things."

She was drying her eyes now and nodding.

"He's right, you know," said Carly. "He really has made himself look stupid. And not just once. In fact, he seems to be quite good at it."

I turned to look at her, with a 'what the hell?' face, but was met by Carly making eyes at me that I understood immediately meant, 'go with it'.

It was working. I didn't really mind being the focus of the joke, if it helped her get through what she was going through. Although I will say, I was still a little confused as to what was going on and quite why we were being so nice and friendly to someone who, until ten minutes ago, appeared to think we were dirt on her shoes. I guessed that it was just another of those 'Year 6 things', where I was being the new me and dealing with it in a more mature manner.

"Thanks… both of you. I don't really deserve you being so nice to me. I've been a right cow…"

And THAT was the moment where there was a huge BANG on the window next to us!

We'd been so focused on what was happening around the table that we'd completely forgotten about what was going on outside the huge picture window next to us in the street. The last time I'd looked, Mr Rawes had been deep in conversation with two police officers and had been trying to talk his way out of trouble. With the arrival of Isabella-Banana (I'm really going to have to shorten that name, it's too long… maybe Banana is better?), we'd been concentrating on understanding the change in personality and how someone, who normally appeared to be such a… well, 'cow', I suppose… could turn into someone, who was so contrite and wounded and in need of a friend.

Anyway, the BANG brought us back to the full picture and was immediately followed by the SMASH of a coffee cup, which Penny was about to put on the table and was now all over the pristine black, shiny floor of Café Olé.

I think she shrieked at the same time.

But not as loud as we three shrieked, when we turned round to see Mr Rawes plastered up against the coffee shop window, with two police officers – one at each side of him – restraining him!

THIRTY-THREE

Kate (Katherine) Delta was born Kate Anderson and grew up with her sister, Julia, in nearby Kirkham, where their dad was the local GP. Unfortunately, he died when mum was about my age, but her mum – my gran – is still alive and it's her that we go to visit on a weekend.

Mum doesn't have an exciting story behind her, like the Delta family, but I do know that they came from Scotland originally. Mum says that she can remember her grandma speaking with a very broad Scottish accent. My gran isn't Scottish, except when it suits, like when England plays against Scotland at football, or rugby – then she's very Scottish. She always has biscuits hidden in her pantry and she always slips me a couple of pound coins, when Mum and Dad aren't looking. Dad says she has a bit of 'the devil' in her, but he says that in a nice way and I think I understand it. She seems very old and sometimes very tired, but she's also very sharp and is quick to wink at me when the occasion arises, like when there's a difference of opinion over what to watch, or who is right in an argument. She always sides with me, probably even when she knows I'm wrong.

She doesn't go out very much, we go to her. Dad's mum and dad are 'quite mobile' according to Mum and Dad, but Gran is pretty much restricted to her house. I don't know if there's a medical reason behind this – I've never asked – it just seems to be the way it is.

Mum spends a lot of time looking after Gran, doing her shopping and visiting her every day.

She's very caring, is Mum.

She doesn't spend much time doing anything if it's not for someone else, so it wasn't a surprise at all when she wrapped Isabella-Banana (or Banana?) in her arms, turning her away from the window and the excitement outside.

I must admit, I was worried that the shop window was going to break. Three bodies pressed up against a piece of glass must be quite a lot of weight. The couple at the next table had stood up and moved away and the shop owner had gone outside to have a go at the police.

Penny had her arm placed protectively over Carly's hand, but I couldn't stop staring at the red face pressed up against the glass.

You know when you push your face against a window, as a laugh, to make someone at the other side laugh? Your nose gets pushed up like a pig and your lips spread out – it's very comical and not at all attractive. That was exactly what Mr Rawes looked like now and he wasn't exactly what you'd call handsome in the first place. I figured Isabella-Banana must get her looks from her mum. Not that I fancied her, you understand? I'm just saying she wasn't ugly.

The police seemed to have done what they needed because as quickly as he was thrust at us, he was pulled away, leaving a bit of a mess of saliva and smearing on the glass. All of a sudden, the window seats didn't have quite the attraction as they had held earlier today. But it was clearly the place to be, if you liked action.

"Don't you worry, love," Mum was saying to Isabella-Banana. "Do you prefer Isabella, or Izzy?"

"I… zzz… y," she managed, between sobs. So that made that easier.

"Right then, Izzy, let's get you out of here. We can go back to ours and give your mum a call, if you like?"

All of a sudden, the sobbing turned into wailing and heads started to spin round, looking at us again.

"I don't think her mum is around, Mrs Delta," said Carly, with a grimace.

But Mum didn't flap.

"Well, that's no problem. We'll make sure Izzy is happy first, then we'll start making some calls."

And with that, we were off. Mum had made a decision. She stood up and headed straight out of the café, arm around Izzy the whole time. Penny went around picking up stray items of clothing and bags and followed her. Carly and I looked at each other, both attempting to understand what had just happened. She shrugged and I found myself doing the same, then we both hurried to catch up.

Outside the café, things seemed to be normal again: no crowds, no police officers and no sign of an angry man in a blue blazer.

I looked all around me, to make sure, then scurried after the others, who were heading for the multi-storey car park.

THIRTY-FOUR

Mum was the perfect person in a crisis. She was calm, she made decisions, she gave people orders and they seemed to follow them.

So, after being sent with Mum's purse to pay the parking, I found myself sat in the passenger seat of our car, with Izzy and Carly in the back, as we headed back to ours.

She told me to get her mobile out of her bag and to text Dad to tell him to put the kettle on and that we were going to be bringing visitors.

I did that and got a reply more or less straight away from Dad.

"He says he's at the Cricks and do you want him to come home?" I asked her.

She tutted.

"That's bloody typical is that! As soon as we leave the house, he's straight down the pub. Brilliant."

I presumed she was talking to herself, so I kept quiet, knowing that I'd be getting further instructions momentarily.

"Tell him not to worry," she said and then she looked over her shoulder, "Are you OK back there, girls?"

"Yeah, fine thanks," replied Carly.

"Yes, I'm OK thanks, too," replied Izzy, then she added, "Thanks for looking out for me."

"Don't you worry about that, love. We'll make sure you're OK. Do you have any brothers, or sisters?"

It occurred to me that I didn't know anything about Izzy. Carly had known about her mum, as I guess you would do at a small school. Everybody must know everybody else's life stories. It had been like that at Horley, but at Netherlea, I realised, much as with Archie, I didn't really know much about my classmates. "I've got one older sister," Izzy said. "But she's away at Uni in Newcastle."

"Oh, that's nice," Mum responded, clearly happy to have some conversation going. "What's she studying?"

"Maths, Mrs Delta."

"Don't bother with the 'Mrs Delta', either of you," she said, looking over her should again. "Call me Kate."

I felt a bit like I wasn't involved in this conversation and, to be honest, I was quite happy about that. I felt like, if I said something, it would disrupt the delicate balance that Mum was working hard to maintain.

So I kept quiet.

"Do you like maths then, Izzy? Like your sister, I mean," Mum continued.

"Erm, not really, Mrs... I mean Kate. I'm not very good at it."

"You are!" said Carly, jumping into the conversation. "You did really well on last year's test. You beat me, anyway."

It was quiet for a moment, then Izzy said, "Well... I'll be honest, I copied some answers off Yusuf; he was sat next to me."

We really were seeing the real Isabella-Jane Rawes today, weren't we?

"Don't worry about it," replied Carly, without missing a beat. "I saw Yusuf copying Jack in spellings just yesterday."

"Really?" I said, jumping in. "If Mr Antinori saw him do that, he'd go mental!"

At that, Mum turned and glared at me.

See!

I told you I needed to keep my mouth shut.

THIRTY-FIVE

Penny was already there, when we got back to ours. She took over from Mum, while Mum got the door unlocked and put some lights on, getting us all inside, shoes off and sat in the living room.

Then, after taking drinks orders – I realised I'd not even touched my caramel macchiato – she backed into the kitchen to talk grown-up talk with Mum.

Everyone seemed to have been ignoring the elephant in the room quite well to this point, but I figured someone had to mention it, so I took a breath and dived in.

"Does your dad get angry like that a lot?"

Izzy was sat on the sofa, with Carly on the seat next to her, but she wasn't able to see the angry, warning eyes that I was being sent because she was in between the two of us.

She began by shaking her head, then breathing out, like it was her last breath.

"It wasn't really his fault," she began. "I wound him up, so that he lost his rag. I don't know what I'm going to do now."

Both Carly and I stayed quiet. To be honest, I didn't really know what to say to that. COULD it have been her fault? He did seem to be quite wound up, yes, but was it OK for your dad to be grabbing at you like that?

I couldn't imagine my dad getting like that. He was pretty angry about the pink knickers thing, but he wouldn't have been physical, or violent towards me, surely?

"I met his new girlfriend last night," she confessed. "And her son."

She paused, shaking her head.

"He'd been buttering me up for the last few days, buying me little gifts and saying I looked nice, stuff like that. Then I found out why. He had a new girlfriend."

I was getting a déjà vu here and it was quite disturbing. I was trying to work out why, but it wouldn't seem to drop into place.

"Has he ever had a girlfriend before, you know, since... your mum?" asked Carly, carefully.

"I think he has, but nobody I've met," she replied. "And then, all of a sudden he drops this bombshell on the way home from school and, oh, by the way, we're going round there tonight."

"Wow!" ventured Carly. "That must have been freaky."

"Very!" agreed Izzy.

Again, I had this niggling feeling at the back of my head, something that I felt like I should know.

At that moment, I heard the back door open and Dad's cheery voice as he came in.

I felt like I should be saying something supportive, but again, I was worried about putting my foot in it. The supportive side of me won out.

"I don't really know what to say," I said. "I can't imagine what you must be going through, but I do know that my mum will try to keep you here and feed you with cake until she's happy that you are ready to leave."

They both laughed at that.

Then Dad's voice came from the kitchen, as he shouted, "You are having a GIRAFFE!"

Clearly, Mum had just filled him in and he was back to worrying about his job.

Izzy looked at me, as she put two and two together at the same time.

"Oh!" she said.

"What?" Carly asked, looking at us both backwards and forwards, palms upwards.

Izzy looked at me, inviting me to explain. "It appears that my dad…" I began, trailing off.

"… works for my dad," finished Izzy.

"Oh!" said Carly.

What a mess.

THIRTY-SIX

"I might have suggested to him that being so selfish was probably why Mum left him," Izzy grimaced.

We all grimaced too. Ouch!

We were in the kitchen now.

Me, Mum, Dad and Izzy.

Penny had made polite noises about leaving us to get on with things – I think that Dad coming in from the pub and blowing his top probably had something to do with it. Izzy had clearly been scared of being shouted at by another angry bloke and wanted to go with Carly and Penny. Penny had been nervous at that and Mum had managed to 'have a word' with Dad and calm him down (there had been a lot of raised voice whispering from the kitchen while the other four of us had stared at each other awkwardly in the living room)

After we'd all said goodbyes and Dad had made himself a brew, while staring out of the window at the back garden for five minutes, here we all were.

I looked at Izzy; she still looked quite fragile, much smaller than when I'd come across her at school, where she appeared powerful and in control. Now she seemed to have no confidence and was scared. I marvelled at how our relationship and my feelings about her had changed in the space of a day, from me despising her and everything she stood for to me worrying about her. I couldn't imagine being in her situation – her mum being 'out of her life' (whatever that meant), her elder sister away at Uni and her dad having been led away by the police. For all she (and we) knew, he could be sat in some prison somewhere. Wouldn't someone somewhere be worried about Izzy and where *she* was?

"Can I just ask?" I began, tentatively, looking at Mum and then Dad for approval.

Dad sighed and nodded. "Go on, son."

"Well, won't someone, somewhere be worried about Izzy and where she is? Shouldn't we be contacting someone?"

Mum started wringing her hands and looked at Dad for an answer. I guess, by that point, Mum's control of the situation was ebbing away.

Dad sat back in his chair and put his arms up to his head, crossing them behind it. "I don't know, Oscar. Maybe. But the main thing is, like your mum has been saying, Izzy is safe and looked after."

He took another breath and carried on, "The way I see it, we've got Izzy's best interests at heart here. I'm an employee of her dad's and you are a school friend. We have some kind of duty of care."

He turned to Izzy. "Izzy, what do you think about me phoning your dad?"

She looked up, alarmed, "And say what?"

Dad glanced over at Mum, who was nodding at him.

"Yes," she said. "That's a great idea. Give him a ring. If there's no answer, just leave a message to say that Izzy is here with Oscar and she can stay as long as she wants."

"What if he does answer?" I asked, looking at Izzy, who was playing with her hair, absent-mindedly swapping strands around and looking between us.

"Tell him I'm sorry," she volunteered, and then added, "… because I am. It's all my fault."

She looked like she might be about to cry again. Mum reached a hand out and placed it over her arm, as she let go of her hair.

"Don't worry, Izzy. It's not your fault. You might have said something without thinking, but it's not enough to cause what… well, what we saw."

Izzy stood up abruptly, the chair making a scraping noise against the kitchen floor as it dragged backwards. I think we were all shocked by the sudden movement, but we didn't have time to react as she headed for the kitchen door.

All at once, she stopped, turning round to face us. "I just want to thank you for being so kind and so helpful. Especially when…" she looked at me now, "… when I've been so horrible. I don't deserve it."

Mum had recovered again now and was stood beside Izzy, putting her arm around her and stroking her shoulder.

"Izzy, you've had a terrible shock. You can't leave, we won't let you. Besides," she said, looking out of the back door, "…it's raining out there and you've only got a t-shirt on."

"But I said some horrible things to him," Izzy said, quietly now. "I told him that his new girlfriend was ugly and that she was only after him for his money." She was crying again now.

"I told him that I thought he was ugly too and that they made a good pair and that I wanted to go and live with Mum. That's when he got angry, but I didn't stop, I just wanted to make him more angry and I don't know why."

The last word came out more like, "Whyyyyy," as she turned, wailing and grabbed hold of Mum, holding her tightly.

Mum looked up at Dad, with tears in her own eyes and, again, I wondered about how you really don't know a person at all, unless you completely understand what is going on in their life.

Izzy was a very fragile person, with no self-confidence, who put on this big image of control, to hide the pain that was going on inside her. How she had managed to make everyone, including me, believe otherwise?

THIRTY-SEVEN

The rest of that evening settled down a bit.

Dad left a message on his boss's (Izzy's dad's) phone, as planned, Mum persuaded Izzy to have a 'nice, relaxing, hot bath' and then we had takeaway pizza in front of the TV. Mum had made up the spare room and it all looked like we had a guest staying.

I kept looking over at Izzy, with her feet tucked up underneath her on the sofa next to Mum. It all seemed so 'normal', yet crazy-weird at the same time.

How would we explain all of this on Monday at school? Would we go back to the way we were before, or would this new relationship take over – like being pretend siblings? How long would Izzy actually be staying here? Would people at school think we were going out? Wait, would Carly think that? Would she be bothered?

Why was I worrying about all of this?

Just as all of this madness was unravelling in my head, I was woken up by a ringing from the kitchen.

"That's your phone, love," Mum said, looking over at Dad.

Dad was already halfway out of his chair anyway and heading for the door. Looking at Izzy, it seemed like she was asleep, with her head lolled to one side. Mum was gazing at her, like a protective mother hen.

I hardly dared breath.

"It's going to be her dad, isn't it, Mum?" I whispered, barely audible over some cooking programme on the TV.

"It'll be what it'll be, Oscar," she replied. "We can't change anything. We can only help out where we can."

Again, I looked at Izzy and wondered about whether this was what it was like to have a sister: worrying about someone?

Mum was straining her head, trying to hear what was going on in the kitchen. All I could hear was Dad's low, rumbling voice, but no decipherable words. He certainly wasn't shouting.

That must be good news, mustn't it?

After what seemed like forever, Dad's head poked around the door. He smiled at me, reassuringly, then beckoned Mum.

As she left the room, they pulled the door to.

I couldn't wait until I was old enough to be part of the important stuff. No matter how much I was growing up, being a Year 6 student, going to a new school and impressing Mum and Dad with how I was maturing, there would always be things that I wasn't old enough for.

Mum had lowered Izzy's head onto the side of the sofa and she was fast on, the excitement of the day obviously having taken its toll on her. She looked nothing like the 'posh girl' from school, who had confronted me outside the toilets.

Wow – that seemed a long time ago!

The door opened and Mum slipped back inside, glancing across at Izzy, then coming over to me, kneeling in front of me.

"That was Izzy's Dad, love," she said, quietly. "He's back home and is really, really grateful to us for bringing her back here."

"What did he say?" I asked her. "Did he give any reasons why he was, you know, like he was?"

Mum smiled at me and brushed some hair across my face, out of my eyes. "I don't know everything, love. Your dad's still talking to him, but he seems to think it's a good idea for Izzy to stay here tonight, then he'll come and pick her up in the morning."

"What? He's coming here?"

I hadn't realised I'd raised my voice, but the thought scared me a bit.

"Ssh! Don't wake her up," Mum said, raising a finger to her lips, then looking round at the sleeping shape on the sofa. "She needs to sleep, bless her."

And then, turning back to me, "Are you happy with her being here?"

"Me?" I asked. "Erm, yes, of course. I just want her to be OK. It was a bit freaky today."

Mum smiled at me, then stood up.

"Yes. It was, love. For all of us. Including your dad. But... as it's turned out, it seems like this might be good thing for us... especially your dad and his relationship with his boss."

THIRTY-EIGHT

Wow, I slept well.

I think it all caught up with me when my head hit the pillow.

Dad had come back in and carried Izzy up to bed. I couldn't help but notice the way that him and Mum kept looking at each other and wondered if they were thinking about the Juliet they never had.

I hoped that Izzy would keep coming back here. It actually felt quite comfortable in an 'OMG, what a weird day!' kind of way.

I heard Mum talking in a quiet voice to Izzy, while I was brushing my teeth, but again, I've no idea what was said.

I did plan to get all the info from them once things calmed down.

Before I lay down, I wondered again whether Carly was imagining what was going on. I hadn't noticed Mum ringing Penny, or anything. I didn't even know whether Carly was staying with her tonight.

I found myself wishing I had Carly's number, so I could ring her and speak to her. But then, I'd need a phone in order to ring her.

Why hadn't I asked for a phone instead of an Xbox?

This was something else I needed to discuss with Mum and Dad.

So much to think about…

And then my head hit the pillow.

THIRTY-NINE

I had a strange dream.

I guess I shouldn't be surprised at this, given that, I'd had a strange weekend. And, I suppose, a strange September.

I woke up on Sunday September 30th feeling like I'd forgotten something, or missed something important. You know the feeling?
It's a bit like when you get to school and – all of sudden – you are filled with dread, because you haven't done your homework and you've just realised, but all your friends have done theirs.

I lay there in bed for a couple of minutes, trying to come round, while mentally going through the chaos that had gone on in the past day. The house was quiet; I couldn't even hear the pipes tapping and gurgling, which meant that Mum and Dad hadn't got up yet, because the first thing they always did was pop the heating on, to 'give the house a warm through', as Mum always said.

I looked at my alarm clock and saw it was still only 5:44 a.m. – very early for me to wake up – so I lay still and tried to go back to sleep.
That was when my dream came back to me.
Or parts of it, anyway.

I know it had Stevie in it, which was odd, because I hadn't had ANY contact with him at all since school had begun. Dad had mentioned him a couple of times, but I'd changed the subject. As far as I was concerned, if he wasn't getting in touch with me, then I wasn't going to get in touch with him. In the dream, he was upset and angry with me, like

119

I'd done something to him, but, as I lay there, I argued with myself that HE was the one who had lied to me.

Anyway, I was sure that he was quite happy with Matt Sanderson and his standoffish mum.

Mrs Barker was in it as well. I was back in her class and trying to apologise for leaving. She also seemed disappointed in me.

Daisy of the pink and orange knickers was there also… and Jess. They both appeared happy that I was disappointing people.

Was I disappointing people?
I couldn't think how I would be.

Maybe my dream was advising me to reach out to the people I'd left behind? Perhaps I'd left something unresolved.

I wondered if I should speak to Carly about it? Or Archie?

Archie… that turned a lightbulb on. Why did I think there was something I'd forgotten to do there?

Being in Year 6 should come with a manual. Life was so simple before.
Now I had so many things going round in my head.

I heard Dad get up and go into the bathroom and wondered how well Izzy had slept in the spare room.
Was she awake?
Was she worried about today?
A new day normally felt so fresh, like you could start again, but – for some reason – today felt ominous…

Again, I couldn't shake the feeling that I'd left something somewhere, or missed something.

Dad was going downstairs now.
The heating would start up in the next minute.

I closed my eyes again and drifted off back to sleep.

FORTY

Dad made pancakes!
Pancakes!

Dad never makes pancakes.
In fact, Dad never makes anything – Mum does ALL the cooking, but that morning Dad made pancakes.

They were actually quite good too.

Not only that, but he sang while he made them.
Mum and I kept staring at each other.
In the end, Izzy asked, "Is everything alright?"
We had to explain the normal state of events and that Dad was pulling out all the stops for his guest.
I think that made her feel quite special. I hope it did, anyway.

I didn't actually get any time on my own to talk to Izzy, until about five minutes before her dad was due to arrive – when Mum and Dad went off to 'smarten themselves up'. Fortunately, I wasn't asked to 'smarten myself up', so I kept quiet.

We were sat alone in the kitchen.
Izzy spoke first.
"This must be, like, really weird for you."
I laughed, "Yeah, it hasn't been a normal weekend, but that's OK. I've actually quite enjoyed it."
She looked at me, wide-eyed, "REALLY?"
I realised how that must have sounded, so I tried to back it off a bit.
"Not in that way. I mean, I didn't enjoy you being upset and all that…"
She looked a bit more relieved.

"But, I'm happy I got to see the *real* you and I'm glad you came here. I think my mum and dad wish you were staying – especially Dad, he's taken a right shine to you!"

Izzy lifted her chin and smiled, "You are really lucky, you know, Oscar. Your mum and dad are so lovely. I'm really jealous."

I didn't really know how to answer that, so I thought I'd just be honest.

"Well, I hope you'll come back here. You know you'll always get pancakes."

She laughed at that and again, I noticed how different she looked – relaxed and 'normal', instead of cocky and arrogant.

"Are you going to be OK?" I asked her. "With your dad and that?"

She looked me full in the eyes and replied, "Yeah, we'll be fine. This kind of thing has happened before. Not, you know, as bad as yesterday, but we've had our ding dongs."

She paused.

And right then, the door bell went… DING DONG!

We both laughed and I started to get up. As I did, she reached out and grabbed my arm, "Thanks again, Oscar. You were amazing, you and Carly, when I really needed a friend. I'm sorry I have been so awful at school."

I smiled at her, as I heard Dad opening the front door, "John! Come on in. I think she's in the kitchen with our Oscar."

FORTY-ONE

Mum and Dad were a bit subdued for the rest of the day, after Izzy and her dad left.

Mr Rawes wasn't as dressed up as I'd seen him in town – he actually looked quite normal, like someone's dad looks – and he didn't have an angry red face. He was very friendly, but not in a false way, and he was obviously very grateful because he turned up with a huge bouquet of flowers for Mum and a bottle of whisky for Dad. He even had a voucher for GAME for me and apologised for it being 'impersonal' but said he didn't want to get me something that I didn't like, or already had, which was very nice of him.

Most impressively, he gave Izzy a really big hug as soon as he entered the room and didn't seem to want to let go. For her part, Izzy was grabbing on as tight as he was, so we all breathed a sigh of relief.

They both said 'thank you' a million times before they left. Izzy made a point of telling Mr Rawes that Dad had made pancakes and Dad looked quite embarrassed, but that just made Mr Rawes even more enthusiastic in his gratitude and he made a promise to get us all round for something to eat.

He did add that he probably wasn't up to Dad's standard as a cook, which made Mum and I share a quick glance and a smile.

When they'd gone, the house all of sudden felt very quiet, like all the air had been sucked out of it, so Mum dealt with that like all adults do in similar occasions. "Right, let's have a brew."

Nobody seemed to know what to do with themselves after that.

Mum started preparing lunch, Dad read the papers and I went up to my room to play on the Xbox, but we didn't really communicate; I think we were all a bit sad, which is strange, because we should have been happy.

I wanted to mention my dream and about needing a phone and I desperately wanted to ask them all about what had gone on with Izzy's dad and what Dad and Mum had talked about in secret the night before, but somehow, it just didn't feel like the time was right.

So we plodded through Sunday.

I had a bath – which is traditional in our house on Sundays – and then we all went to bed.

I thought I heard Mum on the phone while I was in the bath, probably to Penny, but I just let it go.

October tomorrow.

FORTY-TWO

Monday, the first of October.

White rabbits.

A new month, a fresh page and all that.

Dad has already left for work when I came downstairs for breakfast, so I decided to tackle Mum about the phone.

"Mum, I've been thinking…" I began.

"Ye-e-es," she jumped in, thoughtfully.

Parents always seem to know when you want something. It's quite hard to catch them out, or out-smart them. I mean, they must have gone through the same thing with their parents, so perhaps it's like an inbuilt radar, or something? I know it's a long time since they were employing the same tactics, but you have to be really clever and appeal to their adult reasoning. Or… simply flatter them – that often works.

Anyway…

"If I'd have been in the position that Izzy was in on Saturday, then…"

"You don't ever need to think about that," she broke in, interrupting me again.

"But you don't know that!" I insisted.

She gave up what she was doing, preparing my sandwiches for lunch and came to sit down next to me at the table.

"Yes, I do, Oscar. Because neither your dad, or me would ever behave like that." She shuddered for effect.

"I'm pretty sure that Izzy thought the same thing," I said. "But what I couldn't understand was why she didn't have a mobile phone? If she'd had a phone, she could have rung someone."

I was feeling pretty good about how this was panning out…

"She did have a phone."

…Until then.

"What?" I asked her. "I didn't notice her phone."

"She had it in her pocket, because she used Dad's charger when we got back here," Mum answered.

"But…" I was lost for words.

"She actually made a point of saying that it was alright having a mobile, but that she had nobody to call. That was why she was so glad when she saw you."

I was still lost for words.

I didn't know how I was going to get this conversation back on track. But it did make me think, once again, how desperate Izzy must have been. Nobody she could call and the one person that she sees who could possibly help her was a boy from her class that she didn't get on with. Someone she'd had a run in with at school.

She was very brave.

I must have looked a bit dejected and lost in my thoughts – some might say I was daydreaming – because Mum leaned forward and kissed me on the forehead, before standing up.

"We know you need a phone, love. You're going to high school next year and you'll be doing a lot more walking around by yourself, so we need to be able to keep in touch. Your Dad and I have spoken about it and we were always planning to get you a phone for your birthday."

My birthday is only at the end of October, so that was a victory of sorts, but it still seemed like an age away.

My thoughts must have been clear because Mum carried on, "But maybe I can have another chat with your dad. We are both thrilled with how you've settled in at Netherlea.

Your dad told me about Archie and I'm trying to get his mum's number, so I can set something up."

I'd forgotten about that… and Archie; that all seemed such a long time ago now. I smiled at the thought of Archie and his crazy lunches… I wondered what he'd have today?

"We're also glad you have such a lovely friend in Carly – especially as she's Penny's Niece. And it goes without saying that we were very proud of how you helped Izzy."

Me? What did I do?

"But I didn't Mum, that was you and Dad."

She smiled at me, turning back to load up my sandwich box up.

"You did more than you think, love," she said. "That poor girl needed a friend and you welcomed her. We were both happy to do what we could."

I think I heard her voice wobble a bit, as she said the last bit and I thought again about the daughter they never had.

Being in Year 6 was hard, but, I reasoned, being an adult was still clearly a tough gig.

FORTY-THREE

Mum talked about half term in the car on the way to school. Apparently, her and Dad had been thinking about us all going somewhere for a couple of nights. We all liked the east coast – Whitby, Robin Hood's Bay, around there.

She said that it would all be down to how Grandma was and whether Auntie Julia was available to help.

Auntie Julia was a nurse and worked, what Mum called, 'unsociable hours', as well as different shifts, so she never knew when she was around. She lived with her boyfriend, Andy, who she'd been seeing for a while now. He came last Christmas and was quite funny – he knows some magic tricks, mainly cards and it really brought the party to life. You could see that Auntie Julia was proud of him to begin with... then (Dad says) the red hair started to take over and he was told to stop.

When I got out of the car, I saw Yusuf, so I walked in with him. He was all excited about some YouTube channel that he had created and tried to encourage me to follow him and rate some of his videos. I tried to be enthusiastic, but basically, I was watching out for Archie, or Carly... or Izzy.

I was desperate to tell Archie all about the weekend, to catch up with Carly about it and to see how Izzy was.

Again, I wondered about how the new relationship would work. Would Izzy start being nice to everyone? Or just me and Carly? Or would she be back to her normal self? Would the walls have gone up again?

I think Yusuf realised that I wasn't really listening to him, because he drifted away when he saw Greg.

I've not mentioned Greg – he's like Yusuf's sidekick, they go most places together. You could see Yusuf on his own, like just now, but it was very rare to see Greg on his own; it was like he only existed when Yusuf conjured him up.

He was nice enough, don't misunderstand me, but I'd never actually seen him speak without Yusuf there. It was like he was a ventriloquist's dummy and Yusuf was the voice. I'm sure there was more to him than that and maybe it was down to me, not trying to get to know him but, quite frankly, I'd enough going on at that moment.

Once I got into the school-yard, I looked around. I waved at Alex and said hi to Harry, but kept scanning.

I couldn't see Archie anywhere and was just about to go up to join Harry, Jack and Alex, when I saw Carly arriving... WITH Izzy!

They were heading straight towards me, chatting happily, like old friends, when I realised I was TOO excited to see them.

I was at school, for goodness' sake and I had a huge, goofy smile on my face!

So I took a moment to take a breath and gather myself. "Try and act cool," I told myself.

"Hi, Oscar," they both said, in harmony.

"Oh, hey, Carly... Izzy," I replied, remembering my dad's advice (they are just boys, they are just boys).

"We were just saying how we thought we might try to go back to Café Olé next weekend, if you fancy it," Carly said, green eyes flashing.

I must have looked surprised – I *was* surprised – after all, it was the scene of 'the crime' and I couldn't imagine how Izzy could ever go back there without imagining her dad plastered up against the window.

"Yeah," Izzy joined in. "I thought it was only fair that I treat you two to the coffee that you never actually got to drink?"

You had to hand it to her, she really was brave.

Maybe it was the old adage about getting back on the bike (or was it horse?) straightaway, otherwise it becomes too big a task in your mind?

"So, what do you think?" asked Carly.

What did I think?

Hmm... well, I was being asked out to the trendiest coffee shop in town by two of the prettiest girls in my school. What would *YOU* think?

"I think that would be a great idea," I replied. "Do we need to take adults with us, or can we hang out by ourselves?"

I don't really know where that came from, to be honest, but it sounded good to me and they were both looking quite excited at the prospect, as they nodded at each other.

"Yeah, why not?" Izzy smiled. "I'll get my dad to pay. Once he knows you are going to be there, Oscar, it can't fail."

Was it me, or did I notice a change in Carly at that? It was only slight, but her eyes seemed to lose their 'sparkle' for a second.

Was she jealous?

I didn't know whether to be more excited, or a little worried.

Thankfully, Archie arrived at that stage.

He was walking towards us from behind Izzy and Carly. He'd seen me and given me a short wave and a short smile – which seemed to make sense as he was a short guy.

All of a sudden something dropped into place in my head, it just clicked... the thing I'd been reaching for since my strange dream, the thing I'd forgotten.

Archie.

The Friday night thing with his mum and her new boyfriend.

He was almost upon us now.

The curry and *Ferris Bueller's Day Off*.

Carly was turning round, as she'd seen me looking over her shoulder, with my mouth open.

His mum's new boyfriend with his daughter, who was about the same age.

"Hi, Oscar, hi, Carly," Archie greeted us, in his usual deadpan voice.

"Hi, Archie," beamed Carly, as Izzy turned round towards him.

That was when his face dropped and he got the angry look again. I couldn't see Izzy's face, but from her voice, I can only imagine what it looked like.

"Oh GREAT!" she shrieked. "What do YOU want?"

"What do I want?" Archie replied, "Well I don't want you and your stupid dad in my life, that's for sure!"

And with that, he stormed away, just before Izzy stormed away in a similar direction, leaving Carly looking backwards and forwards between me and Izzy and Archie with a confused look on her face.

"Ah!" I managed, before the bell went.

"Ah?" she said. "Ah, what? What just happened?"

"Saved by the bell, eh?" I said, turning towards the door and the smiley greeting of Mrs Johnson.

FORTY-FOUR

Carly wasn't too happy about being left in the lurch, but what could I do?

The bell had gone and, I reasoned, it would take far too long to explain.

To be completely honest, I was still processing the whole thing, but what was clear to me was that Archie's mum was in a relationship with Izzy's dad, which they'd both discovered on Friday night, over a curry and an 1980s film at Archie's house.

By the look on both of their faces and the drama that unfolded on Saturday afternoon in town, where I'd had a ring-side seat, the cosy gathering hadn't gone too well.

Another piece of information that had presented itself was that Izzy's dad was a Man United fan. I made a mental note to make Dad aware of this flaw in his personality.

I had promised to fill Carly in on the whole thing at break time.

Obviously, she still wasn't happy and she made that crystal clear.

But, to be fair to me, I'd only just worked it out even though all the clues had been there for the taking. My mind *had* been attempting to unravel it all – even while I slept, but without success.

I resolved to steer clear of being a detective as a career choice.

As I walked into the classroom, I glanced over at Archie and saw that he had retreated into himself again. He looked angry and a little teary.

I knew from Friday evening's episode outside school that getting him out of this wasn't going to be a quick fix, so I decided to leave him to it, settling instead for giving him a supportive tap on the shoulder as I passed him.

Izzy, similarly, looked on the point of shouting at the next unsuspecting passer-by, but nobody in this classroom would notice the difference anyway, as they'd not been part of the 'inner circle' this last weekend, so I decided not to bother her, reasoning that a playful tap on the shoulder wouldn't be understood in the same way and I didn't want to get yelled at.

Hopefully time would be a healer?

As I got my planner out of my bag and searched for a pencil, I looked around the room. Nobody else seemed to be aware of anything out of the ordinary. I caught Carly's eye and she made a point of looking away in annoyance.

Great! Not even 9:00 a.m. and three people were angry, one of them with me and I hadn't done anything.

The curse of Year 6 was striking again.

I put it down to red hair and began copying the spellings from the board into my planner.

As Mr Antinori did the register, I could see that he had noted both Izzy's and Archie's moods, but, after getting their verbal confirmations that they were 'here', he wisely decided to leave them alone.

Maybe I should consider teaching, now that being a detective was out?

FORTY-FIVE

One thing I haven't shared with you so far is the amount of maths and English that we were now doing in Year 6.

In every other year of my school life, I'd been involved in topics about rainforests, volcanoes, Romans, Vikings and wars. I'd had to come to school dressed as an Egyptian and done lots of craft work, bringing in cardboard boxes to make into fairground rides. I'd played recorders (badly), brass instruments (even more badly) and been to weekly swimming lessons and school walks around the village looking at dry-stone walls and examples of Victorian Britain.

This year, that all seemed to have been replaced by subordinating conjunctions, possessive pronouns and something called the subjunctive tense, which Mr Antinori said was how the Queen spoke, but made absolutely no sense to me whatsoever.

I knew that we had to do SATs tests at the end of Year 6, but I think I'd always known that. It seemed that at Netherlea we'd get to have bacon sandwiches before the tests, so that sounded like something I'd be up for and I was looking forward to it, but Mr Antinori told us, after finishing the register, we'd be doing practice SATs this week, so that we could understand what the tests were like, to prepare us for the real thing in May.

There was no talk of bacon sandwiches, just tests.

I didn't mind tests – I usually did quite well in them and, being honest, it was a break from normal lessons, but the mood in the classroom did change and everybody seemed to get a bit tense.

Mr Antinori told us not to worry about these, as they were only for practise and so that he could see how we were doing so far, but I could see the huge pile of test papers on his desk and couldn't help being a bit worried.

What if I didn't do as well as expected?

I'd done really well in the tests at the end of Year 5 and that was why I was now sat here, instead of still being at Horley Juniors with Stevie and Matt and Gemma.

What if that had been a fluke and I wasn't actually that good?

Mrs Barker had told Mr Antinori how well I'd done, so he was obviously expecting me to do the same.

All of a sudden, I didn't feel very good about this.

I didn't have time to worry about it though, as we had to start moving desks around, so that we were divided up. Some children left the room with Mrs Johnson – Archie being one of them. How was Archie supposed to do well in the mood he was in?

I was allowed to stay at my desk, but I had to move around the edge, so that Harry and I couldn't see each other's answers.

For some bizarre reason, I remembered that Harry and I had talked about getting together out of school, when he was at his mum's. Why hadn't that happened? Had he decided he didn't like me?

Why was I even worrying about that now?

I put it down to the tests stressing me out and tried to clear my mind and concentrate on what Mr Antinori was saying.

"So just write your name on the front of the paper. You don't need to write anything else and don't open it until I say so."

Everyone was silent while he handed out the papers. I wrote my name on the front, but there were boxes for the school name and the date and something called a centre number? Was I supposed to know that? Did he say just to write my name?

I'm sure he did.

Someone at the other side of the room was whispering now and Mr Antinori jumped on it. "WHY are you talking, Yusuf? I've asked for quiet," he boomed.

"Do we need to write the school name, Mr Antinori?" Yusuf asked in a very timid voice. Clearly Yusuf was as nervous as me.

"NO!" Mr Antinori shouted and I saw Jess jump in her chair in front of me. "I've said JUST to write your name. You can ignore everything else."

I could see Harry's hand up now and wondered at the wisdom of poking the bear further. Mr Antinori was getting annoyed and this couldn't help, surely? I tried to catch his eye, before Mr Antinori did, but I was unsuccessful.

"Harry, your hand is up," he pointed out, matter-of-factly.

"Erm, yes. Mr Antinori, what's a centre number because I don't know what it is."

At this, Mr Antinori let out a dramatic breath and strode to the front of the room.

"Everyone put your pencils down now and look at me."

Approximately thirty pencils hit the desks. Apart from Harry's, which rolled off the desk onto the floor. This didn't go unnoticed, but Harry tried to get it back surreptitiously with his foot, hoping that he hadn't been spotted.

"LEAVE it, Harry. Just listen, everybody!"

Everybody listened.

"All you have to do is write your names on the front. Nothing else. I will be marking these tests, so I don't need

137

to know your school name, or your centre number, or the date. Just try to follow instructions, so that we can get this done before it's time to go home."

Wow.

All we'd done so far was write our names and even that was difficult.

All of a sudden, I didn't like tests anymore.

Talk about stress!

FORTY-SIX

By the time break rolled around, all the drama of the weekend was a distant memory, replaced by *what the hell is the present perfect tense?* and *how do I know whether 'before' is being used as a preposition or a subordinating conjunction?*

Mr Antinori had made it clear to use that we weren't supposed to know everything on the test, as we'd only had four weeks of school and he'd repeated that this was very much a practice and not to worry too much about it.

He might as well have spoken to his foot because it was all that anybody spoke about when we left the classroom and walked out onto the playground.

We were five minutes into break when Carly appeared and dragged me away from Jack.

I found myself standing next to a large plastic bin, which was nice, and about twenty small children, who were peeling oranges. I've always struggled to peel oranges, so I was oddly transfixed for a moment. One tiny girl, with her jumper on backwards seemed to have her thumb so far inside the orange that I wondered if we'd need the fire brigade to get it out.

'Hello?"

Carly was stood in front of me, tapping her foot, dramatically.

I was transported back to the job at hand.

"Oh, yes, sorry," I began. "Can I start by saying, in my defence, that I was totally unaware of this until school began. Well, I say I was unaware…" I paused.

I didn't get chance to break for thoughts though, as Carly was too impatient for niceties.

"Look, just tell me what is going on, will you?" she broke in, her eyes flashing in a manner that was a clear warning.

Red hair…

"Right. Well, on Friday Archie told me that his mum had invited her boyfriend and his daughter around for a curry. He was upset about it all, but I tried to point out that it might be a good thing…"

"And?" she prompted, again cutting into my flow.

"Wow! Sorry. I'm trying to tell you what happened, OK?"

Carly took a step backwards and looked up at the sky. "Oscar, just tell me… please…"

"I'm trying, but you keep interrupting," I pointed out. Girls can be so annoying at times!

"OK – I'm sorry, but break will end in five minutes and I'm trying to understand why someone who was so horrible all of her life until Saturday, when all of a sudden she became normal and someone I wanted to be friends with and then this morning was so lovely until all of a sudden… Oh!"

And that was when everything clicked into place for Carly.

"Archie's mum's boyfriend is Izzy's dad, isn't he?"

Bingo.

FORTY-SEVEN

As I was heading back into school, Mr Antinori pulled me to one side away from everyone else, so that nobody could hear us.

"I've noticed you've got quite friendly with Archie recently, Oscar, and I just wanted to say well done. He's someone who really needs a good friend and you're a perfect fit."

What do you say to that?

"Erm, thanks, Mr Antinori. I like Archie, he's a good mate."

We were stood outside the toilets and were momentarily interrupted as Daisy and Jess opened the door, exiting with Izzy. They looked a bit stunned to see us there and were frozen to the spot, looking guilty and expecting Mr Antinori to tell them off for something.

"Hey girls, you can head back into class, don't worry," he smiled as he spoke. "I'll just be a minute; I'm having a quick word with Mr Delta."

They looked relieved for a second, smiling at him, then, once his back was turned as he faced me again, both Jess and Daisy gave me what can only be described as the 'hard eye'. As they opened the door to the class, Izzy quickly looked back at me with worry evident all over her face.

She thought I was talking about her, didn't she?

This wasn't going to be good, was it?

She would be thinking that I'd betrayed her.

Great.

You really can *NOT* do right for doing wrong, can you?

"So," said Mr Antinori, returning me to the conversation at hand, "I wanted to ask you if everything was OK with Archie? He's unusually subdued today. He hardly answered any questions on his test this morning and I'm worried about him."

Why do I keep getting thrust into these positions?

I wanted to be completely honest with Mr Antinori; he really seemed like a good bloke, totally on my side and would only have both Archie's and Izzy's best interests at heart, but part of me also knew that, if I told him everything that was going on, then they'd both get taken out of class and have to talk to learning mentors and Mrs Johnson and that wouldn't help them at all. ESPECIALLY if they hadn't asked for it in the first place.

AND, I'd be the one who had put them in that position.

No thanks.

I took a breath and looked up at my teacher and trusted in my new improved judgement, "Something went on this weekend, Mr Antinori," I began. "But I can't tell you what because it would be betraying the trust of my friends."

His face fell and I could tell that he was going to say something that I wouldn't like, so I continued. "All I can ask is that you give me and my friends a little time to work it all out and I promise you that, if it gets any worse, I'll ask for your help."

"Well…" he began.

So I jumped in again, "I tell you what, Mr Antinori. I'll make it known that you have asked me about it, but I've not told you anything… YET. But that I will tell you if we can't sort it out between us. How does that sound?"

Mr Antinori smiled at me and backed away.

"It sounds to me, Oscar, like you are a perfect friend to have. Let me know when I can help you out."

And with that, he opened the classroom door.

FORTY-EIGHT – The grandma project!

You remember the crazy suggestion that I made about getting our grandmas into school?

The one that Mr Antinori said to leave with him and then it had gone quiet?

The one that I thought wasn't going to happen?

Well...

"Today, I'm going to announce an exciting new project that was suggested by our very own Oscar Delta!"

All heads turned to look at me, as Mr Antinori allowed a pause for effect and I imagined that some of them would be wondering what I had got them into.

"We are going to get as many of your grandparents as possible into school... and we are going to call it the Grand Day In," he announced, as the three words appeared on the SMART board.

"Co-ool!" said someone behind me.

"My gran will love that," gushed Harry next to me.

I even saw Jess and Daisy looking excitedly at each other.

Mr Antinori allowed a bit of general excitement to continue for a minute, then he quietened us down, as he took a question from Carly.

"Yes, Carly."

"Will your grandma be coming in, Mr Antinori?" she asked, excitedly.

"Well..." he began, "... she is very old and doesn't leave the house much, but, yes, I'm going to do all I can to get her in here."

Around me, everyone began to get excited again and I could feel myself smiling as I listened to the general buzz around this idea. Mr Antinori again let this carry on, I guess, building it up, so that we all wanted to do whatever work there was going to be to do.

I looked across at him, as he was talking to Yusuf and laughing. He turned round and caught my eye, then gave me the thumbs up.

This was going to be a fun project.

FORTY-NINE

First of all, we were divided up into groups of four.

There was good news and bad news here.

The good news was, I was with Archie.
The bad news, I was also with Jess and Daisy, who made it extremely clear how they felt about this also, by completely refusing to look at either Archie or me, as we sat down to join their table.

As I looked around, it seemed like Mr Antinori had put everyone with a close friend, and then put the pairs with other pairs that they wouldn't normally work with. I was thrilled to see that Carly was working with Izzy – and they looked really quite happy about that also. They'd been paired up with Yusuf and Greg, which was a lot better than we'd got, but I trusted my teacher.
Maybe this would work out?

The first task was for us all, in our fours, to share information about our grandparents and to write it all down on a very large piece of paper. Mr Antinori said that we could organise it however we wanted and write down anything at all, but the only rule was that we weren't allowed to write anything about our own grandparents – the information had to come out verbally, so that someone else could write it down.

After staring at each other, without speaking, for a couple of minutes, it became obvious that our group was going to struggle to co-operate. The girls were still pretending that we didn't exist and Archie was firmly inside his protective shell.

What had looked like being a fun project had suddenly turned into a nightmare.

Mr Antinori was wandering the room, encouraging the groups and soon got to us.

"Not much going on here, is there?" he asked, looking at us all.

I shrugged my shoulders at him, as if to say, 'What do you expect?' but he wouldn't be beaten and picked up the marker pen, handing it to Daisy.

"Daisy, you have neat writing, why don't you write down all of your grandparents' names?"

"O... K," she replied, without much enthusiasm and then turned to Jess.

"Jess, what are your grandparents called?"

Jess turned her chair, so that she was only facing Daisy and said, "I've got my nanan, Karen and her husband, who's not my real granddad, he's like my mum's step-dad."

"Good," encouraged Mr Antinori. "And what's his name?"

Jess squirmed a little uncomfortably and whispered something that I didn't quite catch, under her breath.

"What's his name?" asked Daisy.

Again, Jess looked flustered and looked at her teacher, as if to ask, 'Do I *really* need to say this?'

We were all staring at her by now.

How bad could this name be?

"He's called Archie, OK? Edward, but my sister and me call him grandpa Archie."

Daisy paused, pen poised, but unsure what to do.

I looked at Archie, who appeared to have woken from his slumber and was smiling.

"WHAT?" asked Jess, raising her voice. "What's wrong with that?"

146

I didn't know what to say. I mean, there was nothing wrong with that, it was just a coincidence and…

"That's funny," exclaimed Archie, all of a sudden.

"WHY?" asked Jess. "Just 'cause he's got the same name as you?"

"No," replied Archie. "Because my gran is called Jess! How mad is THAT?"

It was pretty mad.

Daisy was chewing her nail now, unsure of what to do.

Mr Antinori began clapping. "That's great," he said, drawing attention from all around the room. "That's going to be so perfect when we do the next step. Write it all down, Daisy."

FIFTY

Well, it broke the ice.

Fortunately, Jess saw the funny side and Archie was back in the land of the living. Between the four of us, we managed to get all the names down and even a couple of birthdays.

There were no more coincidences and we broke for lunch all pretty much on good terms with each other.

At one stage Daisy had even smiled in my direction. Then she realised and her mouth snapped back to a grimace.

Lunch was 'awkward'.

There was no way that Archie and Izzy were going to sit together, so that meant Izzy was with Carly (and Jess and Daisy), while I sat with Archie and his usual collection of oddities from his fridge.

He began with about six sticks of celery, which is quite hard to say quickly.

While he was crunching away, I filled him in on Mr Antinori's quizzing after break and how I'd not told him anything. He nodded along to that, until I got to the part where I'd promised to let him know if I couldn't resolve things.

He stopped and held out a half-eaten stick in my direction, using it as a prop.

"Well, I'm not going to be making friends with her, if that's what you mean." And pointing his stick over at the table where the girls were all sat, he continued, "I can't even understand why Carly is friendly with her anyway. Last week we were all calling her Isabella-Banana and laughing at her. So why are they so buddy-buddy all of a sudden?"

I couldn't imagine for one moment that Archie was going to find any story that ended with Izzy sleeping in the spare room at my house to be acceptable, so I just shrugged and took a bite of my sandwich (roast beef and mustard, in case you are bothered).

He went back to demolishing his celery and we were dragged into a conversation by Alex, who was sat next to us and wanted to know if we'd watched *Dr Who* last night.

Now, I don't know if you are a fan and I'd like to support the new Doctor, especially as she's a Yorkshire lass, but I just didn't get it. I didn't find it scary and the special effects looked cheesy.

Archie was clearly a fan, so I let them get on with it and went back to my sandwiches.

We were carrying on with the Grand Day In project after lunch, so I got to thinking about that and wondered what *the next step* would be. Mr Antinori had been quite excited about it.

He was quite excited about all of it and I felt pretty proud of my involvement. I just hoped that he could get his grandma into school; that would be pretty special.

Alex was standing up now and saying 'seeya' to people, as he departed. I still had my yoghurt. Archie was reaching for a red pepper.

A red pepper!

"So," I began, taking a deep breath, "it didn't go well on Friday then?"

Archie coughed a laugh out, then took a bite. I could see all the little seeds inside the pepper. Surely he wasn't going to eat *those*, was he?

"I didn't mind the film," he said, between mouthfuls. "But the company was terrible."

"How about the curry?" I asked him, as nonchalantly as possible.

I had him talking now and wanted him to carry on.

"It was OK."

I kept quiet, on purpose, so that he might feel like he should keep talking and, sure enough, "I just couldn't believe that *SHE* turned up. I mean, it's bad enough that Mum has to have a boyfriend at all, but to have chosen someone with *HER* as a daughter! Just… EUCK!"

He didn't have anything further to say.

I didn't know how I was supposed to sort this out. I just hoped that Carly was having more luck.

FIFTY-ONE (The next step)

"Now you've all started to get to know the grandparents on your tables, we are going to move onto the next step."

Mr Antinori paused again, for effect.

He seemed to be getting quite good at this. I wondered if he was rehearsing for a spot on the *Great British Bake Off*.

He cleared his throat.

"You are going to write invitations to the grandparents on your table. To ALL the grandparents on your table... EXCEPT your own."

Eh?

We were all doing that thing again, where we looked at each other questioningly.

"Yes," he carried on, "... that's right. So, Alex, for example, will be writing to Jack, Heidi and Emma's grandparents. Whereas Heidi will be writing to Alex, Jack and Emma's grandparents."

This was confusing.

People started to put their hands up.

"Yes, Harry?"

Harry looked about as confused as I felt.

"So, what do we write? I mean, I've never met the other grandparents on my table. How will they know who I am?"

Mr Antinori smiled, as if everyone had fallen into his trap.

"Exactly, Harry," he replied. "Which is why you have all begun to write things down on your tables about these people. The next step is for you all to share your favourite memory of something that you did with your grandparent, which will give you more to write about. I also want to know what they do, or did for jobs? What are their hobbies? Favourite programmes? We are going to build a fact-file for every grandparent in this class, so that when you write to them, you can include whichever of these facts YOU think is interesting to you and why YOU would like to meet them. When we get our visitors into school and we have our Grand Day In, I would like us all to be looking forward to meeting new people and making new friends."

He really had thought this through, hadn't he?

This was going to be amazing. I felt quite excited about it all.

Looking around, other people seemed to be feeling the same as I did.

"Yes, Izzy."

"Who will write to your grandma, Mr Antinori?" Izzy asked.

"Great question, Izzy," he replied. "I'm going to select people based on their enthusiasm, their involvement in the project and the letters that they have written. They will be given the opportunity to write to my gran."

And just like that, the competition was on.

FIFTY-TWO

"Is there any way that I can ring Carly?" I asked Mum, on the way home in the car.

I'd explained the Grand Day In to her and she thought it was a fantastic idea, although she did caution against me getting too excited about Grandma coming into school. She said it was more likely that Dad's mum and dad would be able to make it, but it would depend on their 'trips'.

They did take a lot of 'trips' – Dad always joked that they were never at home and they joked back that they were trying to spend his inheritance.

He'd tried to explain that to me once, but I found it confusing. It was *their* money, after all, so how could it be *his* inheritance?

He'd told me that he completely agreed and we left it at that.

Maybe it was one of those 'adult' things that were best left alone?

Mum pulled into the driveway and turned to me, smiling. "I don't see why I can't have a word with Penny. Maybe she can give Sarah and Craig a ring and see if it's OK."

I was guessing that they were Carly's mum and dad.

She didn't ask what I wanted to talk to her about and I didn't feel like explaining, so we left it at that. I headed up to my room to get changed and, when I came back downstairs, Mum was on the phone with Penny, saying her goodbyes.

I tried to act like I wasn't bothered, when all I wanted to do was ask her what she'd said and I think Mum knew that and strung me along for a while, by asking me if I wanted a drink and, "Was I hungry? Because it would be a while yet before Dad got home."

In the end, I caved first and asked her whether that was Penny on the phone, which I obviously knew it was.

Mum met me halfway, thankfully and told me that Penny was going to get Carly to call me.

I tried not to be too excited... but I was.

Even though the reason I wanted to talk to her was nothing to do with 'us', still I had butterflies in my tummy – a bit like I had on Saturday morning, when we were driving into town, but more so. Talking over a phone isn't like talking face-to-face. Every word was important, because the other person was going to be listening intently to what you were saying. It was easier to make a complete idiot out of yourself.

I'd never spoken to Gemma (the only other person, who could have been considered a 'girlfriend') on the phone. In fact, the only girl I'd ever spoken to on a telephone was my uncle Matt's stepdaughter, Ali. She was a few years older than me – about fourteen – and was quite cool. The last time I'd met her, when Uncle Matt was having a garden party, to show off his bar/shed, she'd had about three friends with her. They were all tall and pretty and there was no way at all that I would ever dare talk to them. She went to Holmdale High and Mum and Dad had engineered it so that she would ring me to tell me how much she enjoyed it. This was near the beginning of the summer, when we were just getting over the big fall out, after the trip to Florida. It had been the most awkward conversation in the world, with me barely saying anything. In fact, I had said one thing, which still made me cringe and I'd lay awake at night thinking about it for weeks afterwards. When Ali had asked me if I had any questions about anything at Holmdale, I asked her if you were allowed to go to the toilet during lessons.

I mean... what kind of an idiot asks questions like that?

This was precisely why I was getting worked up over speaking to Carly.

To make things worse, the phone didn't ring for all the next hour and then Dad got home, which meant Mum told him about Carly ringing, which made things worse and then the phone didn't ring again and then we were sitting down to eat.

And then... obviously... the phone rang.

FIFTY-THREE

I had my fork poised, pasta heading for my mouth: my first bite.

What would you have done?

Sorry if I let you down.

I put my fork down and looked at mum, inquiringly, seeking permission to answer the phone.

Mum and Dad were looking at each other, sharing another one of those adult 'moments' and then, after what seemed like an age, Dad said, "The phone's ringing, Oscar. You'd best get it before she hangs up!"

I didn't need telling twice.

Abandoning my meatballs and pasta (which, by the way, I really enjoy), I scooped up the phone off the kitchen work surface and headed out of the kitchen, into the hallway, pressing the green phone button as I did.

Then, as it connected, I took a deep breath, tried to steady my nerves and said, "Hello?"

"Hi, Oscar, it's Carly."

Why did she sound so much more relaxed than me? Was she relaxed, or was she feeling exactly the same as I was? Was the only reason that she'd waited so long to call because she'd spent an hour or more trying to calm down?

"Oscar? Are you there?"

Oops – that'll be me daydreaming again!

"Hi, Carly. Sorry, I was just making sure that Mum and Dad weren't listening in."

She laughed. That sing-song laugh.

I realised that I was going to have to be the one to speak here; it *was* me that set this up, after all.

The sing-song laugh had given me confidence, so I went for it…

"So, Mr Antinori spoke to me this morning, outside class."

"Yes, Izzy told me that she'd seen that," Carly replied straightaway. "She was worried about what you were telling him."

"Well, I didn't tell him anything, so she needn't be worried."

"I told her that, Oscar. I think she knows that, but she was just scared that everyone would be taking Archie's side of things."

I'd not thought of that.

I told Carly exactly what had gone on in the conversation and how we'd left it, so that I'd more or less promised to 'solve' things, or go back to him to seek help.

"Right," she breathed into the phone. "So, what you're saying is that somehow, we need to make it so that Archie and Izzy can get on with each other?"

"Yeah," I replied. "Sounds easy, doesn't it?"

Cue sing-song laugh again.

I laughed along with it.

I told her about how stubborn Archie was at lunchtime and filled her in on his take on how it had gone on Friday night.

"Yeah," she agreed. "Izzy was the same, but it didn't help that Jess and Daisy kept chipping in. They really are a bad influence on her!"

"Which is strange," I jumped in, "…because they were actually getting on with Archie by the end of the project today. Maybe they just like the drama?"

"Oh yeah. Totally!" she agreed.

We both went silent for a moment, thinking.

"So what do we do?" I asked.

"How long have we got before Mr A wants to know what's going on?"

Hold up.

"Mr A?"

"Mr Antinori!" she answered.

"Well, yeah. I realised that," I said. "I just didn't know that we were calling him Mr A. How long has that been going on?"

"Longer than you calling Izzy, Isabella-Banana, and far more sensibly," she replied – a little more quickly than I had expected. But still, quite amusing.

"OK... point made. But I don't call her that now."

"Does Archie know that?"

Huh?

I didn't get it. Where was she going now? "Does Archie know what?" I asked her.

"Does he know that you no longer call her Isabella-Banana and that you are now friendly with her?"

"NO!" I said, raising my voice, then a little quieter, in case Mum and Dad had overheard. "No, he doesn't. Can you imagine what that would do to him? And anyway, he has noticed that you are – all of a sudden – bosom buddies with Izzy, Daisy and Jess."

"Ah," she responded.

"Yes, ah."

Then I had a thought.

"Wait a minute. Is there any way that we can use this new project and Jess and Daisy working with me and Archie to help us?"

It went quiet for a moment.

"Well, I'm not sure how," she finally replied. "But it's the only idea so far. Is there any way that you could get Archie to come to town on Saturday?"

I thought about it.

"Yes. I think I might be able to. We have been talking about getting together. But won't he freak out when he sees why he's there?"

"Maybe. But he might behave differently outside school. It's worth trying. And, in the meantime, I'll try to get Izzy on her own and talk to her. But you might want to think about telling him about last Saturday before he finds out."

That was a good point.

That really wouldn't be good, if he heard it from someone else first.

"OK," I said. "But you need to let Izzy know about what *Mister A* said."

She agreed that she would do that.

We had a brief chat about the project and we both discussed how excited we were and how we both wanted to be able to write to Mr Anti— sorry, Mr A's grandma.

Then the door to the kitchen opened and Mum looked out, to tell me that I needed to get my tea.

"I need to go now, Carly," I said. "So I'll see you at school tomorrow."

"Yeah, OK. See you Oscar."

And with that she was gone.

The meatballs tasted lovely. I didn't even notice whether they were warm or cold.

FIFTY-FOUR

Day two of the practice SATs – Reading!

I was sat on the short edge of the desk again, but this time – along with everyone else – filling in the front of the paper didn't faze me.

I was, however, fazed by the *size* of the paper. Mr A (I'm doing it now) had already told us that we had an hour (AN HOUR!) for this test. It seemed to me to be both a long time to be doing a test and also not long enough for the amount of paper I had on my desk.
    Stress day number two!

The day had begun well enough: Mum had asked me to get Archie's phone number, so she could ring his mum, as she hadn't been able to find it through the three other mums she knew. I'd asked Archie before school and he'd given it me straight away. Archie, it appeared, had his own mobile already. He whipped it straight out and read his mum's number to me, which I then WROTE DOWN WITH A PENCIL because I'm from the 1980s and don't have my own phone! Thankfully, Archie was sympathetic and didn't say anything.
    So, I'd put it in my planner and was already planning to get Mum to ring his mum tonight. I'd mentioned about going into town to Café Olé and he was up for it.

Now all I needed to do was figure out how to break it to him that we were double dating and he was fixed up with his mum's boyfriend's daughter.
    There were no scenarios where I could see that working out well.

Izzy had said hi to me as she entered the class and Archie hadn't noticed, which was good, but Daisy had and had made a point of looking wide-eyed and shocked, before scowling at me.

So, clearly working with her most of yesterday hadn't softened her opinion of me. I was going to have to put on a serious charm offensive. But I wasn't too optimistic of my chances there either.

Talking of optimism, back to the reading paper.

Mr A finished his instructions by telling us that we were all very good at reading and we just needed to make sure that we managed our time well.

Hmm…

As it turned out, I needn't have worried; I finished the paper with almost ten minutes to spare and managed to check through most of my answers (YES… I checked them!) before we were told to put our pencils down.

Going out to break, I felt quite smug, which was probably why I decided to take the bull by the horns when I realised I was walking alongside Daisy.

"How did you think it went?" I asked her.

"Oh, it was OK to begin wi—"

She was already part way through answering before she realised that she was talking to me and I think that she was so shocked that she didn't know what to do, so she carried on, "…with, crm… I mean, the panda bit was OK."

I jumped in, to keep the conversation going, "Yeah, I thought that. The second text wasn't bad either. Did you finish?"

We were walking and talking. I could see that she was frantically looking around her for the safety of Jess, or Izzy, but because they weren't there, she had no alternative but to talk to me.

"I just got to the end, when he said we had one minute left. I didn't get much chance to check, but… you know?"

"Yeah, better than you thought, with the size of the book?"

"YEAH!" she agreed.

I was even reading her thoughts now.

I decided to go one step further and to take the high moral ground.

"Daisy, can I just apologise for... well, you know. It really was an accident and I'm sorry if I upset you. I didn't mean it."

She was flabbergasted. Her eyes were doing the wide-eye thing again. I wondered if she was flashing back to lying on the floor, showing me her knickers and being embarrassed.

I, for one, was trying hard not to remember either incident and hoping, with fingers and everything crossed that this was going to be a positive outcome.

"Erm... OK. Thanks," she managed and then Jess dropped into stride alongside us, so I thought I'd quit while I was ahead.

"Great. Well I'll see you in English then."

And I headed off to find Archie, leaving a confused Jess to grill her friend.

One down... one to go.

FIFTY-FIVE

I didn't find Archie; it turned out that he gets extra time for tests, which meant he missed the entire break.

I was worrying that this might have a bad influence on his attitude, but I couldn't have been more wrong as he skipped into English and sat down, just as I was arriving.

"Mrs Johnson gave us some wine gums," he said, with a huge grin.

"What are wine gums?" asked Daisy.

I had thought that he was talking to me, but it was great to see Daisy joining in. I was just thinking of a response that would encourage her more, when – surprise, surprise, Jess got involved.

"Oh! I love wine gums."

"What's your favourite colour?" I asked her.

"Red," she replied. "What's yours?"

This was going so well!

"I really like the white… not the yellow, but the white."

"White?" Archie exclaimed. "I've not seen any white ones?"

"Are we ready over there?" asked Mr Antinori, but really meaning, 'Shut up over there'.

We all shared a conspiratorial smile, then got back to the task at hand.

Mr A gave us all A4 grids of paper, which had boxes to fill in with titles such as: hobbies, favourite memory and interesting facts. We were to carry on the work yesterday, but to gather all the information from the large sheets of paper and organise them onto the smaller grids, to make it easier to see.

After that, we began drafting persuasive letters, using formal writing, but including personal information.

It was actually much more fun than it sounds and it involved a lot more discussion and chatting within the group.

By lunchtime, I was amazed at how much we'd got done, but – more importantly – how much we'd all got on in our group. Archie, in particular, had been a star and Mr A made a point of singling him out for praise in front of the class for his enthusiasm.

Once again, I made a mental note… I MUST tell Archie about Izzy before it's too late.

FIFTY-SIX (The night of two phone calls – call one)

I gave Mum Archie's mum's number as soon as I got in the car and she said she'd ring her after tea.

Tea turned out to be just Mum and me, as Dad was working late with what Mum called, 'some high pressure, new important customer', so we picked up some fish and chips on the way home.

There's a great chippy near Horley High school, where they give you free chips if you order a fish butty. I'm sure that other people must know about this, but it always seems like it's our secret. The woman there always looks at you and does the 'shh!' finger to her mouth, then turns round to make sure the bloke on the fryer isn't looking, before she loads a scoop of chips into your butty.

They taste amazing!

Anyway, we took them home and put our own salt and vinegar on (in case other people think we put too much on and look at us disapprovingly), then eat them out of the paper, but ON plates.

Crazy, huh?

That's how we roll.

Don't tell dad, he'd flip out and want to know why we don't just use one or the other.

Sometimes it's nice to break with rules and conventions.

I was just tidying up when the phone rang. Mum got it and then said, with a smile, "It's *CARLY,* Oscar," as she passed me the phone.

I took the phone out in the hallway again and pulled the kitchen door closed.

"Hey, Carly."

"Hi!" she sang. "I just wanted to let you know that I spoke with Izzy today and she'd totally understood about the Mr A thing."

"Did you tell her that I didn't tell him anything?" I asked her.

"Yeah, she was fine. I knew she would be. But she's a bit unsure where we go from here. She's not upset with Archie, or anything, but she says she's not crawling to him either."

I understood what she meant. I wouldn't want to do that either.

"Well, Archie is up for Saturday," I told her. "But exactly how I'm going to go about breaking it to him about Izzy being involved, I don't know. And it also occurred to me that I should fill him in about last weekend, in case someone does that before I do. That really would make things a nightmare."

"I spoke to Izzy about that," she jumped in. "She said that she wouldn't say anything and that she hadn't even told Daisy or Jess."

Phew! What a relief!

"Wow! Well then, I wonder if I even need to tell him? What do you think?"

She was quiet for a second.

I was getting used to her quiet pauses now, so I waited. "Hmm," she began. "I don't know. It could work, but then if he finds out later, he'll wonder what kind of a friend you are."

"Yeah, but if I tell him now, he might not be my friend any longer anyway!" I suggested.

As it turned out, I needn't have worried. The decision had been taken out of my hands.

FIFTY-SEVEN (The night of two phone calls – call two)

Carly pretty much had to go after that. Apparently, her dad had arrived home and she had to get off the phone because it was 'time to eat'.

I popped the phone back in the kitchen and thanked Mum for tea, then decided to have a bit of Xbox time. Before I went, Mum said that she'd give Archie's mum a bell and asked me what time did I want to get together with him on Saturday?

I told her about the plans to go into town and she suggested that she pick him up just after lunch, then drop us both in town. She said that she could do some shopping while I was there and pick us up later.

It all sounded perfect. Well... apart from the Archie and Izzy thing.

I was just heading up to my room, when I heard Mum say, "Hi, is that Archie's mum?"

Do you stop and listen in to conversations like that? I decided to.

It was about *me* after all, so it couldn't be rude, could it?

I sat on the stairs and cocked an ear towards the kitchen.

"Oh!" said Mum, in a sympathetic voice.

Straightaway, that got me worrying.

"Oh... Yes... I see... Oh dear," she said.

Maybe I should have gone upstairs. Listening to this side of the phone call, it didn't sound good. What could have happened?

"No. Don't worry… No, it's not your fault… You were doing what you thought was right, he's your son, after all."

I didn't dare move. What had happened?

"Why don't we say that the offer stands and if they manage to sort it out before then, we'll go ahead with it?"

Then, "O…K… I'll let Oscar know… Well, of course, he'll be upset… No, no, don't worry… These things have a way of working themselves out."

Basically, after that Mum gave Archie's mum her number, wished her well and said goodbye.

I was still sat on the stairs when Mum came looking for me.

She was about to shout up to my bedroom, with her hand on the bannister, looking up to the top of the stairs, when she noticed me sat there.

"Oh, hello love. What are you doing sat there?"

I told her that I'd been halfway up, when I'd heard her on the phone and had stopped because it had sounded so strange.

"Yes, love," she said, joining me on the stairs. "There is a bit of a problem."

I said nothing, waiting for her to carry on.

I noticed, as I sat there, gazing over Mum's shoulder, at the window by the door, that the street light outside our house was flickering. It's funny when you notice such unimportant things at these times. I mean, I didn't even know there *was* a streetlight outside our house!

Anyway…

"It seems that Izzy's dad had told her all about what happened at the weekend. You can understand why… it must have been quite an upsetting event for him."

"O… K…" I said, already dreading what was coming next.

She'd told Archie, hadn't she?

"So, in an effort to get Archie to understand how this was affecting everyone else and not just him – is he a little... sensitive, Archie?"

"What? Oh, yes. Yes... He's had quite an emotional time over the last few years – his dad died at work."

"Oh, how awful," Mum sympathised.

"So, she told him about Izzy sleeping here, didn't she, Mum?"

"Yes. She said that he was quite upset about it, love. I don't really know him, but I can see how that might affect someone who's been through what he's been through."

Great.

This wasn't good.

"Yes," I agreed. "He's probably really fallen out with me."

"She was very apologetic, love. She said that she wouldn't have said anything if she'd known that he would react like that."

I could see that I was going to have to speak to Mr Antinori tomorrow.

"I'm sorry love," Mum said.

"Don't worry, Mum," I replied. "I'll sort it out."

And, for some reason, I really believed I would.

FIFTY-EIGHT (Night owls)

The dream came back again during the night.

This time there was no Mrs Barker, but Stevie was there and he was with Gemma. They were in the shop, where I'd seen him with Matt, during the summer.

I was following them around the shop, up and down aisles full of boxes. They knew I was there and they were laughing and having fun at my expense, but I couldn't get them to turn around and acknowledge me.

They wouldn't talk to me, no matter how much I tried.

Finally, in desperation, I cut around some shelves and sprinted forwards, so that I could try ahead of them, but when I got round the corner, they'd already turned around and were going back the other way.

It was all very frustrating.

So frustrating that it woke me up.

It was dark outside and my clock said 3:14 a.m.

I tried to get back to sleep, but I was too wound up, so – in the end – I went downstairs and got a glass of water.

I thought I'd been quiet, but when I turned round, Dad was walking into the kitchen, looking concerned.

"Are you OK, son?"

I wondered when he'd stopped calling me hero.

"Yeah, I just had a bad dream…" I told him, "… and I couldn't get back to sleep, so I thought I'd get a drink. I'm sorry if I woke you."

He ruffled my hair as he reached into the cupboard for a cup and flicked the kettle on.

"Nah. I was awake anyway," he replied. "We've got a new contract at work and there's a lot to think about. It could mean big changes. And I mean BIG! I think my mind must be working as overtime as I am."

He plonked a tea bag in his cup and went to the cutlery drawer to get a spoon.

"How's Izzy doing?" he asked.

I sighed involuntarily, as the kettle boiled. The steam pouring out of the kettle mirroring my breath.

"Oh! That bad, eh?"

"No, not really," I said. "It's just my mate Archie. You know, the one you met outside school last week?'

"Yeah," he responded, pouring the boiling water into his cup. "He seemed like a nice lad."

"He is," I replied. "But he's had a lot to cope with in the last year, or so and he's a bit sensitive."

He nodded at me to go on, as he sat down at the table.

I pulled out a chair opposite him, quite liking this father and son chat in the middle of the night. I felt quite grown up.

Not so long ago, I'd have been given a cuddle and despatched off to bed and now here I was, swapping stories with my old man in the wee small hours.

"Well, last Friday he was worried about his mum, because she'd invited her boyfriend round and he wasn't right happy for lots of reasons. Then, believe it or not, her boyfriend turned out to be your boss!"

Dad's face was a picture.

He was literally about to take a swig of his tea, but ended up putting his cup back down on the table and staring at me.

His mouth hung open.

"Yeah, Dad. That's what I thought! But it gets worse. You see, nobody liked Izzy at this point, because she acted all posh and stuck up and none of us realised that this was an act because she was unhappy. So then she turns up at his house with her dad and they both freak out and then this week I've been trying to be sympathetic with him,

171

because I feel sorry for him – I mean, his dad was a fireman and he died – but at the same time I'm trying to be friendly with Izzy, because I feel sorry for her and, it turns out, she's a pretty nice girl and then tonight he found out from his mum that Izzy stayed here last weekend and now he thinks he's got no friends and, well… things are in a bit of a mess really."

We both stared at each other for what seemed like twenty minutes, but was probably only thirty seconds, then Dad just said, "Wow!"

It was quiet again.

We went back to sitting and staring. Dad took the sip of his brew and nodded his head wisely.

"That makes my work problem seem like nothing, Oscar," he finally said.

I didn't say anything; I just took a sip of water.

"The thing is, son. You are doing the right thing by Izzy and you are trying to do the right thing by your mate Archie and sometimes you just can't please everyone."

"Yeah, but I should have told Archie about last weekend," I said, sighing.

"And would Archie have liked that?" he asked. "I mean, would he have said, 'Thanks for telling me that, Oscar.'"

"Definitely not."

"Well then… how about this: we both go back to bed now and then, tomorrow morning, we get up and I take you round to Archie's house before school and you try to straighten things out with him?"

I sat back in my chair and thought.

"He won't talk to me, Dad."

"He'll have to do if you go and knock on his door, Oscar. I can take you early, before he's ready to leave. I'm sure his mum will let you in, then you can tell him the truth. Tell him why you didn't tell him before now and tell him that you wouldn't be there if you weren't his friend and didn't want to make things right."

At half past three in the morning, it sounded like quite a good plan.
And it was the best idea we had.

We shook hands, I told him thanks and we both headed back upstairs to bed.

"Night, son," he whispered.
"Night, Dad."

FIFTY-NINE

We realised, over breakfast, that none of us knew where Archie lived, so Mum offered to ring his mum and let her in on the secret.

Thankfully, she thought it was a superb idea, so – before I knew it – I was sat outside Archie's house in the car with Dad.

"Remind me again, why am I doing this, Dad?"

Dad reached over and put a large paw on my shoulder, then leaned forward and looked me in the eyes, 'Because you are a hero, who does the right thing and fights for his friends."

It worked.

Archie's mum had been expecting me, so she let me in quietly and led me through a hallway to their kitchen.

Their house was a bit smaller than ours, but it was warm and cosy, if a little manic. It felt like the people who lived here dashed about, picking things up and putting things down. There were a lot of 'things' around: jackets, shoes, magazines, bags.

Archie's mum wasn't small, like Archie, but neither was she tall. She was squirrelly-looking (in the nicest possible way), with short cut brown hair, which you could tell was done in a salon – not your mum's friend's kitchen, and very smart clothes. I guessed that she must have an important job in an office somewhere.

She told me to call her Jo, poured me a glass of orange and invited me to sit at the kitchen counter.

They didn't have a kitchen table, but they did have a large island, which floated free of the kitchen worktops, with high stools around it.

Most of the stools had piles of books, or magazines on them, but I found one that didn't, which faced the kitchen doorway, that I'd just come through.

I was just sitting down when I heard noises above me.

"That's Archie now," said his mum quietly. "He'll be down any second. Can I just say, Oscar, that I think it's very brave what you are doing. I know what my son is like and this might not go as well as we both hope, but inside he will appreciate this and, in his own way, it will make him realise how much of a friend you are... it just might take him a bit of time."

I didn't think she needed me to reply, so I just smiled (or was it grimaced) back at her, to show her that I completely understood.

The noise was coming down some stairs now. I remembered seeing them facing me when I'd come in the front door, so I was expecting his shape in the doorway almost exactly when I saw it.

He didn't exactly look happy when he entered the kitchen, but – credit to him – he didn't register surprise, or shock, he just carried on with what must have been his daily routine, walking past me to a kitchen cupboard. I heard him rummaging about and the clunk of crockery before he returned with a bowl. He went away again and I heard a fridge door open and then close, then I could hear him rattling cutlery around.

In all this time, his mum said nothing and I just sat there, holding my glass of juice, while Archie stacked his breakfast things opposite me.

Finally, he came back with a box of Rice Krispies and climbed up onto the stool.

He put the box down on the table and looked at me, then the unexpected happened... he smiled.

"Morning, Archie," I said, trying to make this seem like it was normal, like I was always sat here when he came down for his breakfast.

He just shook his head and began pouring cereal.

"Well, I'm off to work," announced his mum, picking up one of the bags.

I wondered briefly how she knew which was the right bag and if she ever got to work to find that she hadn't got what she needed? Maybe they all had the same essentials inside?

"Have a lovely day and don't forget to lock up."

She kissed Archie on the top of the head, as he poured his milk. "You too, Mum, and I won't," he replied.

Then she came around behind me and kissed me on top of the head too. "Lovely to finally meet you, Oscar. See you again soon, eh?"

"Thanks Mrs Ker— erm Jo," I stammered. "I hope you have a nice day."

Then she picked up a bunch of keys, waved from the doorway and was gone.

Isn't it interesting how we all live different lives?

SIXTY

I told Archie the whole story, while he munched away.

He never once interrupted, asked any questions, or showed any kind of emotion – disappointment, anger, or anything and I wondered if this is what happens to you when you lose a parent.

I didn't know for a second what it must be like, but I could imagine that the feelings would probably be so strong at times, that showing them, or getting them out safely would be impossible. I could see why Archie had become like he was. He'd become an island; a bit like the one we were sat at, keeping all of his emotions to himself, hiding them away.

It couldn't be good for you and I hoped that I was helping, being a bit of a bridge to the island.

Wow, Mrs Barker would love the metaphors here!

Archie finished his cereal and cleared up, putting his dish and spoon in the dishwasher and cereal in the cupboard. Then he put the milk in the fridge and came out with a green pepper, a couple of carrots and a large tomato, all of which he put into the usual plastic tub. He then threw the tub into his bag, which was under the table.

"I'm just off to clean my teeth," he announced and tramped out of the room. Then I heard his footsteps disappearing up the stairs.

I looked around the room again, noticing the clock on the wall and was astonished to see that it was 8:35 a.m. and realised that I'd been here almost half an hour!

School would be starting in fifteen minutes.

How did Archie do this every morning, getting his breakfast and to school on time without someone behind him? He was actually more independent than I was, I marvelled.

"Come on then," he beckoned from the doorway. "Or we'll be late for school."

SIXTY-ONE

We appeared to be OK now.

Walking round to school from Archie's house, he began to talk about the two maths papers that Mr A had told us we'd be doing that morning, so we'd obviously moved on and there seemed to be no lasting effects, which was a result, but… I still had to tell him about the plans for Café Olé and who would be there.

"So, are you up for this Saturday then, Archie?" I asked him.
"Yeah," he replied. "What are we up to, again?"
  "Well my mum's off into town and she said she'd give us a lift if we fancied it, so I thought we could go to Café Olé."
  "Ah! The scene of the crime."
He smiled wickedly and did a bit of a Bond villain cackle.

Deep breath.
  "Yeah, actually Izzy might be there with Carly. Would that be a problem?"

I was learning to understand Archie a bit better now. And, as usual, he didn't miss a beat, he just kept walking alongside me, with no sign of any problem, but I knew, inside, he was processing and contemplating.
  Eventually, as we arrived at the school gates, he replied, "Nah. As long as I'm not paying."

Say what you want, he is hilarious.

SIXTY-TWO

The first maths paper was totally easy and I went out for break, feeling great about everything.

Carly fell into step, as I walked onto the playground.

"Hi," she said. "That was OK, wasn't it?"

"Yeah," I agreed. "I was pretty shocked how easy it was. I bet the next one won't be as easy."

"Have you decided what you are going to do about Archie?" she asked.

"Oh wow! You don't know, do you?" I exclaimed and I spend the next five minutes bringing her up to date with the current dramas in my life.

Unlike my dad, she *did* interrupt throughout, peppering me with questions and adding the odd involuntary noise, like 'Oh' and 'No way!'

"So he's happy with us all going to Café Olé together?" she finally asked.

"Well, I wouldn't say he's exactly *happy*," I told her. "But he's OK with it taking place. What does Izzy think about him coming along?"

She looked down at her feet and shifted, uncomfortably, before looking back up at me, with a very guilty look on her face.

"Oh no! Don't tell me... you haven't told her, have you?"

"Well... not exactly, no," she admitted.

My expression must have given away what I was thinking because she went on the defence immediately.

"Look, it hasn't come up, OK? I'm not really sure if she's totally ok with me inviting you, never mind Archie."

"Hang on a minute!" I broke in. "Invited *ME*? I thought it was *us* that were going in the first place and everyone else was invited afterwards?"

"OK!" she replied, raising her voice. "SORRY! I didn't realise I needed your permission on how to do things. Maybe it would be just easier if I went with Izzy and you went with your friend, Archie."

It wasn't a question.

It was a statement.

And with that, she walked away, leaving me wondering what had happened and whether I had been part of it.

SIXTY-THREE

Just when I sort one relationship out, another one breaks.

It reminded me of a guy I once saw on TV spinning plates on sticks. He was dashing backwards and forwards, trying to keep them all going, but there was always one that needed attention.

Maybe life was like that, I wondered, instead of concentrating on the maths paper in front of me.

I had been right, this one *was* a nightmare. There seemed to be loads of stuff on it that I'd never come across before. I'd answered about ten questions, but there were twenty-two altogether and, no matter how much I looked at some of them, I couldn't seem to understand what on earth I was supposed to do.

Maybe it was the red hair?

One thing was for sure, the solution was not going to be to chase after Carly – I knew for a fact that this would only make things worse. It would be like the first week in school all over again.

Besides, as usual, I hadn't actually done anything wrong, had I?

I tried to get my mind back on the maths paper, but it was hard. Maybe the bad night's sleep was also catching up with me?

Then Mr Antinori was at my side.

He knelt down, large black beard level with my desk.

"Everything OK, Oscar?" he said softly, so nobody else could hear.

Have I mentioned how much I like my teacher? I think I probably have.

"Some of these questions are confusing," I told him. "I can't seem to understand how to do them."

He smiled at me; even his dark eyes appeared to be smiling.

"Oscar, don't worry, it's not your fault. You haven't been taught a lot of this yet, so I don't expect you to get one hundred per cent correct. Just read them through, think about what you *do* know and see whether that helps. Do what you can. OK?"

"OK, Mr Antinori," I said. "Thanks."

He put his hand on my arm, reassuringly, for a moment, then departed.

For some reason, my teacher's supportive gesture awakened something inside of me and, reading the paper through again, I *did* see places where I knew relevant facts and I made sense of the wording in some questions, which I hadn't previously.

Sometimes it's not *what* a teacher teaches you, it's *how* they teach you.

SIXTY-FOUR

We were well on with the letters to grandparents now.

Mr A had asked us all to write what he called a 'generic' letter; one that could be sent to anyone's grandparent, inviting them into school and giving them information in order to be able to do that – like the date... that was important. I say that because Alex had missed that on his letter. And then, once we all had our 'generic' letters drafted in our literacy books, we had to use them and add the personal details that we'd collected, to be able to write to individual people.

So far, I'd done my letters to Archie's grandma (his mum's mum) and was now writing to his gran and granddad on his dad's side. They lived in the Republic of Ireland and Archie hadn't seen them for a long time. I wondered if it was since his dad died, but didn't ask him. I guess visiting relatives is a two-way thing and, unless Archie and his mum made trips to Ireland, then why would they see each other. After all, they were the older ones – I didn't know exactly *how* old – and they couldn't be expected to be popping over to visit once a week.

He'd spoken about them in his usual resigned manner and it was hard to tell what he really thought, but I'd made it a personal quest that I wanted my letter to be the reason for them to visit.

So I was putting my all into it.

He'd told me about a memory he had of when he visited them one Christmas, with his mum and dad and how he'd woken up one morning in a large bed, with one of their dogs lying on top of him, keeping him warm. Later that day, they'd all gone out for a snowy walk and he'd ridden on his granddad's shoulders. He remembered being around a table with lots of people and his gran's laughter. He couldn't remember how old he was, but it was the most Archie had ever told me and he'd seemed (if it was possible) even further away behind his eyes, while he talked.

I tried to put it all in and carefully checked all my spellings and grammar.

Archie had rattled off letters to my gran (Mum's mum) *AND* my gran and granddad on my dad's side and was at the front of the room, showing them to Mr A, when we were brought to a stop.

"I just want to announce who I'm asking to write to my gran," Mr A said, standing up and clapping his hands together dramatically. "But first, I'd like to tell you all how proud I am of how you've embraced this project and the effort that the you are putting into it. I know, when the day itself arrives, it will be a massive success."

We all positively glowed. I bet you could have used the energy in the room to power the school at that point.

"So… this has been a very difficult decision, but I'm going to ask two people to stay in tomorrow break, so that I can share my memories with them, in order that they can write to my gran and those two people are…"

Don't you love a dramatic pause?

I'm actually overdoing it here, but it's working, isn't it?
I wonder who you are guessing he picked?

"… Archie and Izzy."

SIXTY-FIVE

There was no telephone call from Carly that night.

I was slightly disappointed because I hoped she might at least ring to clear the air, even if she wasn't going to apologise.

I honestly didn't dwell over it though and, the next day at school, I didn't pay her any attention. It wasn't that I was *ignoring* her, I just didn't really see her, except in class, but we were doing tests then, or finishing letters – Mrs Johnson was posting them out at the end of the day – so our paths never crossed.

Archie stayed in at break with Izzy and, incredibly, appeared very excited about the whole thing. At lunchtime, he even mentioned Izzy's name twice – in between crunches, as he devoured a gigantic yellow pepper!

During the afternoon, they actually sat together, as they finished their letters – it was all very unexpected, but quite lovely.

For my part, I got another letter done – this one to Daisy's nan.

I'm always interested in people having a 'nan', as opposed to a 'gran' and can't help but wonder whether I've missed out on something. Nan sounds more affectionate – *are* they getting more love and affection? I don't know.

Anyway, I thought I wrote a lovely letter and it certainly made Daisy smile.

And... then it was Friday!

SIXTY-SIX (And… then it was Friday!)

Mum dropped me off at the usual spot – not outside Archie's – and I was just turning around after waving goodbye when Carly walked up to me.

"Hi," she said, sheepishly. "Are you OK?"

It was early and I wasn't sure how to gauge this conversation, so I just went back to dad's advice (treating her like any other boy).

"Hi, Carly. I'm good. You?"

"Not bad. Better now the tests are over. Do you think we'll get some results today?"

We were walking through the school gates now, amongst the usual throng of parents and children, so I waited until we'd cleared the crowd, before continuing with the conversation, "I hope so. Mr A did say that we'd be going through a couple of them."

And so it went on. Not a word of what had gone on; we were picking up as if nothing had happened. I decided that was probably a good idea. I certainly didn't want to provoke anything – there was no way I was bringing up Saturday before she did.

And she didn't.

The bell went, we wandered inside and the day began.
Confusing.

We did get the GPS papers back, during the first lesson and I was chuffed to find that I'd made the pass-mark, as had several others. Harry asked if we still needed to do the test in May and got a stare from Mr A, which was a reasonable answer.

Mrs Johnson told us all that she had posted off the letters, so all we needed to do was wait for replies to roll in. She did make it clear that they'd gone second class – cutbacks, apparently.

As I was going out for break, Mr A stopped me and asked if we could have a 'catch up'. Once everyone disappeared, he asked how Archie was doing.

"Yeah, I think he's doing fine now, Mr Antinori," I replied.

I still wasn't comfortable calling him Mr A to his face.

"Can I ask you something, Oscar?"

Oh dear. What was this going to be?

"Erm, yes," I said, in a voice that gave away that I really wasn't comfortable with where this was going.

He chuckled.

"Don't worry. I was just going to ask if the problem that Archie had on Monday – was it between him and another girl in this class?"

I thought I could answer this without giving too much away.

"Yes," I told him.

"And would I be correct in thinking that this girl was a girl who you had a run in with at the start of the year and who has, remarkably, completely changed her attitude this week?"

Again, I felt like I was on safe ground.

"Erm, yes. That's right, Mr Antinori," I replied.

"Well then, Oscar, I just want to say how impressed I am with how you are affecting people in a positive way and I want you to know that I've recommended you to Mrs Hall for a school award and I'll be sending a postcard home to your parents."

I should say here that Mrs Hall was the headteacher. I still had a problem remembering her name, but here it was.

I wasn't sure how to respond.

I was proud and thrilled and I knew my parents would feel exactly the same, but I've never been good at accepting praise, so I mumbled a "Thank you, Mr Antinori."

And then, after thinking for a second, added, "But you have to accept some of the praise too. You supported me, so thank you too."

I can't be sure, but I think Mr A looked quite emotional.

He didn't speak, he just nodded, wisely and turned back to his desk.

SIXTY-SEVEN (And then it was Friday – part 2)

The bell had gone and I was just coming back into school with Archie when I thought I saw Mr Antinori in the school car park, but I dismissed it because, well… he was my teacher and he was supposed to be in my classroom during school time, not in the car park.

The problem was, he wasn't.
And, it *had* been him in the car park.

And now Mrs Hall was stood at the front of the classroom. It was a good job that Mr A had only just reminded me what she was called.

We filed in quietly, partly because we were confused and partly because it was the headteacher… here… in our class.
This wasn't the usual state of affairs.

She tried to smile, awkwardly, at us, I guessed to reassure us and try to build a relationship, but I think we all just knew that something was wrong.

"Hello, Class 6," she began, as the last person – Greg – took his seat. "This is a nice opportunity for me to get to see you all, but unfortunately it's on a sad note, as Mr Antinori has had to leave for the day."

I glanced around the room to find that everyone else was doing the same thing. We were all catching each other's eyes and trying to see if anyone else seemed to understand what was happening.
'Why was it sad?' I wanted to ask.

Fortunately, in a class of thirty-two children, there's always going to be someone who will ask the question that others are scared to tackle.

This time, incredibly, it was Archie, who put his hand up.

Mrs Hall looked as disbelieving as we all felt. She'd been head for a few years now, so I'm sure she was well aware of how introverted Archie had been.

"Um, yes... Archie?" she asked.

"Why has he had to leave? Has something bad happened?"

It was immediately obvious, by the look on her face, that it had. She cleared her throat and launched into it, "Mr Antinori wanted me to apologise to you on his behalf. He didn't want to upset you all, especially as he's told me how hard you've all been working."

She paused here for a moment.

"There's no easy way to say this, but his grandma has passed away this morning."

I've often heard the expression 'you could have cut the atmosphere with a knife' – Mrs Barker used it to explain idioms – but I'd never actually experienced it until then.

SIXTY-EIGHT

I was still upset when I got home.

I didn't cry – although I was one of the only ones who didn't. Greg cried buckets!

Archie, obviously, didn't cry at all, but he went into his familiar mode.

I didn't see Carly cry, but she was upset.

Mrs Hall was actually very good.

She said some lovely things about how his grandma had lived such a long time and how we'd all helped Mr A to come up with the Grand Day In idea and how this could now be in her honour.

She said that we would all need to look after our teacher and make sure he understood how much we cared about him.

That helped to get a few more crying.

Mum said that Gran had already received one letter from Archie and one from Jess and that she had really been excited about it. Apparently, she was dead set on coming into school, but Mum said that she wasn't sure it was a great idea.

I didn't fight her on it – I didn't have the energy – but I thought that I'd mention it again this weekend, when the time was right.

I hadn't spoken again to Carly about Saturday and Café Olé, so I didn't know what time her and Izzy were going, or – indeed – if I was welcome along. Instead, I'd arranged with Archie that we were picking him up just after 1:00 p.m.

Then, out of the blue, she rang.

"Hi, Oscar," she said. She sounded like I felt.

"Hey, Carly. Are you OK?"

"I'm quite sad about Mr A's grandma. It doesn't really seem fair that we get all this organised and then she dies and misses it all. Maybe we should be cancelling it, in tribute?"

"I don't know," I replied. "I thought what Mrs Hall said was spot on. This should be in her honour and we should get make sure that she gets talked about. It would be nice if we could get some photos of her."

"Hmm…"

She was sounding interested now.

"That sounds lovely, Oscar, but how do we get them without asking Mr A and I don't know about you, but it's going to be hard enough looking at him without crying, never mind asking him about his gran."

I thought for a moment.

While I was thinking, she continued.

"So, are you and Archie coming tomorrow then?"

Huh?

Are you following?

Was this a girl thing?

A redhead thing?

I decided to keep using my dad's tactics.

"I thought you didn't want me to come?"

She laughed.

"Don't be silly, Oscar. I didn't *mean* it."

She could have fooled me.

But what did I know? I was a ten-year-old kid, who was wading through the deep waters of Year 6. Every time I thought I was in a beautiful, blue, clear stretch of water, I came across some seaweed, or a jellyfish.

I wondered if I'd ever reach the beach?

I hope Mrs Barker is reading this.

Instead of saying all of that and coming across as stupid, I simply said, "Well... Archie and I were thinking about going in around half one, if you want to join us?"

I was pretty proud of that one.
 Even more proud when she said they'd see us then.

SIXTY-NINE

Archie and I walked in there at 1:35 p.m.

We didn't *plan* to be 'fashionably late' – that was down to Mum's parking problems – but I'm going to go out on a limb and say that it didn't hurt.

Archie was in what could only be described as one of his buoyant moods. (I once heard Auntie Julia use that expression and looked it up. It said, 'you feel cheerful and behave in a lively way'.)

It captured him perfectly; he had a broad grin and was making sarcastic comments.

Incredibly, Carly and Izzy were sat in the same booth at the window that we'd been in the Saturday before. I could only imagine the bad memories that this must have brought back when Izzy sat down, but when we walked in her and Carly were laughing out loud at something, so she must have shaken it off.

We walked over to where they were sat and all said our hellos.

They had already got what looked like a hot chocolate each, which was confirmed when Archie asked, "Is that hot chocolate?"

"Yeah," Izzy replied. "It's delicious. Do you want some?"

He stopped in his tracks at that.

"Are you asking me if I want to take a drink from your hot chocolate?" he asked with incredulity.

"Oh yeah… Probably not then," she replied and we all laughed – including Archie.

"Don't worry. I don't want to catch your germs anyway," he told her with a grin. "I'm going to get my own. AND a chocolate muffin!"

"Why?" Carly asked, with a grin of her own. "Don't they sell green peppers here?"

He nodded as we all laughed again.

"I *ONLY* eat fruit and veg in the week. On a weekend, I live on chocolate, crisps and pizza."

"And curry," Izzy broke in, with a grin of her own.

Archie broke into a round of applause at that one and we all laughed again. AGAIN! This was really going so well.

In the end, Archie got his chocolate, I got my caramel macchiato (FINALLY) and we both had a chocolate muffin.

I paid.

Archie did offer to split it, but Mum had given me ten pounds, so I was feeling generous.

We sat together, quietly, as we all munched away: Archie with chocolate all around his mouth.

Then Izzy broke the silence, "Well... at least the view is better this week! It's nice to be able to see the high street without some red, sweaty bloke blocking the way."

I almost choked on my muffin, with laughter.

Carly winked at me across the table and, again, I marvelled at the twists and turns in my Year 6 life.

I appeared to have quite a lovely set of friends.

Even if they did all have quirks.

SEVENTY

All in all, it was a good weekend, despite Mr A's grandma passing away.

Mum and Dad spent a bit of time talking to me about it all. I never knew Mum's dad and both Dad's parents were alive and holidaying, so I'd never encountered any death at all.

We hadn't even ever had a pet, so I'd not been upset over the death of Tiddles, or Rover.

I didn't really know how to 'be' about it all, to be honest. I mean, I had never actually met her and Mr A had only mentioned her two or three times in passing. I was more sad for my teacher than anything and Mum and Dad were both very supportive about that. Mum had bought a plant from Marks and Spencer – which is, apparently, a very nice shop in town and I planned to give it to Mr A on Monday.

I was sure I wouldn't be the only person 'showing their support' – as Mrs Hall had put it – in that way.

Archie had come back to mine after we'd been in town and we'd played on the Xbox and had some pizza for tea, then his mum had picked him up. When I had answered the door, she'd reminded me to call her Jo, so I'd introduced her to Mum and they'd got on like a house on fire (another of the phrases Auntie Julia uses).

She'd ended up coming in and having a glass of wine with Mum, which suited all of us: Archie and I had another hour on the Xbox and Dad had slipped away to the Cricketers.

That night I had been revisited by my recurring dream, but this time it ended happily. I was in the shop again and this time Stevie was with Matt Sanderson, Gemma and Mrs Barker. They were all talking and laughing, but I quickly realised that I wasn't alone. Archie was there and Carly and Izzy, then at the end of the dream, Mr Antinori turned up. The next time I looked around, Stevie and the others were gone.

I lay awake thinking about it for a while after I woke up.

Did it mean that I'd now 'moved on'?
Was I now a fully-fledged Netherlea student, with my own friends and my own teacher?

I hoped so.

SEVENTY-ONE

Monday morning.

Mum insisted on coming into school with me and made us go in early. I argued about it for some time, without any success. She said she'd spoken to Jo (Archie's mum) and they'd both agreed that they wanted to show their support as parents also.

I was worried that I'd look silly and tried to tell Mum that this was going to end up being about me, when it should be about Mr Antinori and his grandma.

I needn't have worried.

I thought *we'd* got there early, arriving ten minutes before school, but the area outside the classroom was already full – of my classmates AND their parents.

Izzy was there with her dad, who made a point of coming over and shaking my hand, before speaking to mum.

We met Carly's mum, Sarah (who was also a redhead) and she was soon gossiping away with mum about Penny, while Jo stood there laughing.

Everyone seemed to have a gift and we were all enjoying ourselves, which was ironic really when you think about *why* we were all there.

It was almost as if we were all there for a party, when, in reality, our teacher's grandma had died.

In the end, Mrs Johnson opened the door early – way before the bell and invited us all in.

We all shuffled into the classroom and didn't really know what to do. Part of me wanted to sit in my seat, part of me wanted to stay with mum, but my overwhelming urge was to go to my teacher, which I did.

I started a bit of a trend.

Whilst the parents stood back, one by one, all of us, Mr Antinori's class, walked up to the front of the room. Mum had given me the plant, which I handed to Mr A.

"Thank you, Oscar. That's very kind," he said. "My daughter loves plants, so I might put this in her bedroom."

I didn't really know what to say and I hadn't prepared anything for such an occasion, so I just opened my mouth and found myself saying, "I'm really sorry about your gran, Mr Antinori."

He put the plant down on his desk and turned back to me, putting both of his huge hands onto my shoulders, before saying, "I know you are, Oscar. But I got to spend a long part of my life with her and, most importantly, I got to take her some cake – which she really enjoyed. It was the most excited I'd seen her in a long time, so… thank you, Oscar Delta. None of this would have happened without you."

I smiled at him and he winked at me as he turned to greet Alex, who was next in line.

I found my way back to Mum, who was stood there with tears in her eyes.

"I'm very proud of you, son," she said.

SEVENTY-TWO (Anna's Grand Day In)

The Grand Day In was renamed Anna's Grand Day In after Mr A's grandma and Mum had finally relented, agreeing to bring my grandma in, but she 'wouldn't be staying long!'

The idea was that we would begin school as normal and get things set up, with the grand-parents arriving from 10:00 a.m.

There was a huge buzz in the classroom during registration and I could see that Mr A wanted to calm us down, but at the same time didn't want to dampen our enthusiasm.

All around me, my friends were chatting excitedly about the imminent arrival of their family members; there wasn't one person who didn't have someone coming in... except Mr A. I looked across at him, sat at his desk. He was propping his head up with his elbows as he glanced around the room at us all. He appeared to be happy, but who knows what goes on behind someone's eyes?

What they are thinking...

I decided to find out, so I stood up and wandered over.

"Hello, Oscar," he said as he sat up and his eyes brightened.

"Hello, Mr Antinori... do you mind if I call you Mr A?"

He laughed.

"No, Oscar, I don't mind in the slightest."

I knew that I was wanting to say something, but I didn't know what, so I kind of loitered, bouncing from one foot to the other.

"Is there anything else that I can help you with, this morning?" he asked.

When I looked at his face again, I realised that he had trimmed his beard a bit; it seemed more, I don't know, square? Does that sound right?

I must have been staring at it, with a puzzled look on my face, because the next thing he said was, "I had a go at it with some scissors before my gran's funeral. I think I made a bit of a mess of it, to be honest and I did consider shaving it all off, but I've kind of forgotten what my face looks like without it and was worried it might scare you all."

I smiled at him.

"You can't cut if off, Mr A. It's part of what makes you you."

He nodded.

"I thought so too."

I couldn't think of what to say. I knew there was something, but I couldn't dislodge it from my brain, so I just stood there some more.

I must have looked a bit daft and a few people had started to notice me. Archie was looking over with a confused expression on his face. I tried to reassure him by doing that over-exaggerated smile thing, where you don't actually open your mouth, but his eyebrows knitted together over the tops of his eyes and his forehead creased, so I'm guessing he didn't understand me.

"You know, Oscar," Mr A said, after a few more seconds that felt like minutes, "I'm OK. It's nice of you to be concerned about me, but I'm OK."

He'd read my mind and made it so easy for me because he'd understood exactly why I was hovering around his desk.

I felt the presence of others around me, but I'd decided what I wanted to say now, so I pressed on.

"Today there'll be lots of grans and granddads here, Mr A. It might be a bit upsetting for you at times and I just wanted to say that if you want to borrow my gran for a bit, you can."

His eyes twinkled again and looked so shiny that I felt like I could see myself in them. I wondered later if there had been moisture in them. It wasn't wrong to cry; it made you human, Mum says.

"Mine too," said Izzy suddenly from beside me.

"And mine," said Carly, who was behind her.

"My gran smells a bit…" Archie said "… *and* she sometimes takes her teeth out to eat, but she tells very funny jokes and you are welcome to borrow her for as long as you want."

SEVENTY-THREE

Gran stayed for over an hour in the end and spoke to nearly everyone in the class – even people I'd never said more than two words to!

She spoke to Mr A, although she seemed a bit unsure who he was – I think the beard put her off – and she was determined that Mrs Johnson was my teacher. He tried very hard, but in the end, he looked at me, grinned and shrugged his shoulders.

Archie made sure to speak to Archie (Jess's grandad) and, of course Jess sat with Jess (Archie's grandma). Despite the smell, which Archie had mentioned – and I'm fairly sure he was exaggerating here – and her taking her teeth out – which she did, when she ate a biscuit – Jess was with her for quite a long time.

Most of the grans and granddads (and nans) spent their time sat down, drinking cups of tea, which Mrs Hall and Mrs Johnson kept bringing in.

We all got to eat loads of biscuits, which was epic. Most were a bit boring and plain; there were *some* chocolate ones, but Greg ate most of those! Mr A had to take him on one side and have a word with him at one point.

Archie's mum was there, with Jess (his grandma) and she sat with my mum. They'd become quite friendly in the past couple of weeks and were even planning to go out for a 'girls' night out', which was unheard of. There was talk of Penny and Sarah (Carly's mum) going along too. Dad was thrilled with it all. Mum said that this was because he wouldn't feel guilty about going out with his mates. Dad didn't reply to that.

I'd never heard back from Archie's dad's parents, which had disappointed me, but Archie had accepted it in his usual way, letting it simply roll off him.

I wondered if it hurt him inside.

I hoped that he'd see them again one day.

My gran and grandpa Delta had rung our house one night last week – they gave their apologies, but said they'd be in Croatia on holiday. Dad had rolled his eyes when I told him, muttering, "Typical!" and walking away chuckling.

I wasn't too disappointed; I knew that would be the story.

This was all far bigger than I'd ever expected; a room full of my class-mates with their grandparents, all sharing stories and memories, all smiling and laughing and making new friends.

"This is ace, isn't it?" Carly asked me.

I was stood in the middle of the room, just taking it all in. I nodded in reply, her question not really needing a verbal response.

"And to think," she continued. "It all happened because of you."

She turned – her red hair flying – looked at me and smiled, her green eyes flashing.

Those green eyes.

I realised that I hadn't daydreamed for ages. Maybe things were finally settling down?

"Not only me," I finally replied. "I couldn't have done anything without my friends."

I thought back to week one, when it had all seemed so frightening, when I hadn't known anybody and every small thing had appeared like a huge deal.

The new teacher with the huge beard, Daisy's pink knickers and getting into trouble at school, then at home.

Quiet Archie, who shouted out in class had become my best friend. He was still a work in progress, but he was my friend.

Isabella-Banana had gone from being posh and annoying, to being just Izzy, a sensitive, amusing girl.

Carly had gone from being a redhead with an unpredictable temper to... well, to be honest, she hadn't changed at all.

And she still had those green eyes.

"What are you thinking about, stood there with that smile on your face?" she asked me, wrinkling her nose up.

"LO: To understand green eyes," I replied and I laughed.

She laughed along, in her sing-song way.

"Ooh, what a lovely laugh you've got, young lady," said my gran, approaching us with mum holding her arm to steady her.

"Really?" asked Carly.

"Yes," said Gran. "It's like a melodic tune. I could sing along, if I knew the words."

"This is Carly, Gran," I told her, introducing my friend. "Carly, meet my grandma."

Gran reached out her thin hand to grasp Carly's and looked carefully up into her face.

"Why, what beautiful green eyes you have. Have you seen her eyes, Oscar?"

I laughed again.

"I have, Grandma. I have," I replied.

SEVENTY-FOUR

The main course came out with a bit of a fanfare.

Dad had told Luigi that it was my birthday and he knew that I always ordered the lasagne, so they made a point of putting some candles in the top.

Of a lasagne!

Ever seen that before?

No.

Me either.

We were at Aldo's, celebrating my eleventh birthday. Me, Mum, Dad and Archie.

It was a Friday night, no school tomorrow and things were great.

I looked down at my new phone, a Samsung S7 Edge, for the hundredth time that evening.

It was Dad's old one, but I didn't care. It was my first phone – a smartphone, with loads of cool apps and games on it.

I only had a few numbers in it – but they were important ones: Mum, Dad, Auntie Julia, Archie, Izzy and, of course, Carly.

"Put it away now, son," said Mum, after she'd carefully removed eleven candles from my main course. "You don't want to get bechamel sauce all over it, do you?"

"No! You don't," agreed Archie. "*AND* it's very rude to have your phone out at the table!"

He grinned away to himself as he picked up a slice of pizza, which was the same size as his head.

I shook my head, tucked my phone in my pocket and dived in to the lasagne.

Mmmm…

"What are you going to do with your birthday money then, son?" asked Dad, while shovelling a fork full of spaghetti carbonara into his mouth.

I'd got £20 from Auntie Julia, another £10 from Gran and then an envelope had arrived today from Gran and Granddad Delta with £40 in it!

Forty pounds!

Dad was livid. "Who sends cash through the post?" he'd demanded. "Anyone at the post office could have helped themselves to that! Senile, they are! Going stark, raving bonkers!"

I think Mum was just concerned that Dad might go the same way, as she stood there raising her eyebrows in exasperation.

So… seventy pounds to spend.

What could I spend it on?

"Well…" I began, blowing on my food, to cool it down. "… I think a new game for the Xbox could be in order. There are a few new ones out."

"Black Ops!" shrieked Archie. "Get that, then we can play together online."

"That's not one of those horrible ones, where you go around shooting people, is it?" asked Mum, who had already eaten half of her calzone. She's got an asbestos mouth, apparently.

I'm not sure what asbestos is, but this expression is another one of Auntie Julia's.

"Erm!" replied Archie, with a grin. "Maybe…"

Mum looked across at Dad, for support, only to find him winking at me.

Busted!

"Tony!" she exclaimed, with mock horror.

At least I think it was mock horror – there may have been a bit of concern in there – but it was enough to bring Dad back on her team.

"Your mum's right, son," he agreed. "We don't want you playing something that's not age appropriate. But..." he glanced across at Mum again, "... we'll have a look at it. Sometimes there are settings aren't there? So you can change the game to different levels?"

"That's right, Mr Delta," Archie said. "You can switch off the blood and guts, so it's not as gory."

"Charming!" was Mum's only response.

At that moment, my phone dinged.

Well, there were only six possibles and three were sat here with me.

I turned to Mum for her OK.

"O...K... Seeing as it's your birthday."

"It might be Auntie Julia," I told her. I did text her earlier, to thank her for the birthday money.

Dad began asking Archie more about the settings on Black Ops, while I ferreted my phone out. I swiped the screen to unlock it and saw, to my happiness, that I had received a message from Carly.

I clicked on it to open it.

"Fancy Café Olé tomorrow?" it read.

Everyone else appeared distracted, so I quickly responded, "Defo. What time?"

"In my day, we only had Streetfighter," Dad was lamenting.

"What's that?" asked Archie.

Mum was shaking her head.

DING!

They all turned to look at me, so I ignored them and opened the next message.

"Shape of things to come!" muttered mum.

"1:30?"

"Mum," I began. "Could I go into town tomorrow?"

"Oh yeah…" said Archie. "Don't tell me, let me guess… Green eyes?"
    "Green eyes?" said both Mum and Dad together.

Archie was grinning silently, loving it all.

"Who's green… wait a minute, your gran said something… ah!" said Mum, as the light bulb went on.
    Archie just sat there, nodding.

"Of course you can, love," Mum responded, with a big smile.
    She turned to dad, who lifted his head and shrugged his shoulders, as if to say, 'What am I missing?'
    "You'll give him a lift into town won't you Tony? So he can meet Carly."
    "Of course I can!" said Dad, winking at me again.

Archie was still nodding with a big daft grin on his face.

"See you there," I typed and returned to my lasagne.

SEVENTY-FIVE

So, that's how I managed Year 6.

Well, the start of it anyway.

I was under no illusions that there would be dramas to come, especially with the friends I had.

But the irony was, I'd be able to cope with them, *because* of the friends I had.

I knew the SATs were on the horizon, but after the first practice tests, I didn't think that I'd have much trouble.

And… with the teacher that I had… well, let's just say, I was confident.

During the October holidays, I made a point of telling Mum and Dad how much I appreciated them moving me to Netherlea and I apologised to them for the fuss that I'd made during the summer.

We'd just been to a party for Dad's boss. It was at their/Izzy's house and both Mum and Dad had been absolutely thrilled to see her.

Dad had given her a hug, which was very un-Dad.

Archie had been there too, with his mum, who now seemed to be seeing a lot of Izzy's dad and nobody was upset about it anymore – so that was progress too.

Izzy had invited Carly, as well as Jess and Daisy.

They had a lovely house, with a huge 'games room' over the garage, where we all hung out and played pool, listened to music and talked about 'stuff'.

We didn't get home until after ten, which was unheard of; Mum and Dad always like to be home around nine.

I wondered if it was because I was getting older?

Or maybe that it was Dad's boss and he didn't want to be rude?

Or perhaps it was because Mum was best mates with Jo (Archie's mum) and they were chatting?

Whatever it was, I was very happy. I'd had about four cokes and loads of crisps (but not as many as Archie – I don't know where he puts it) and again was feeling quite grown up.

I remembered when I had first made the conscious decision to be 'grown up', to say mature things, that would make Mum and Dad proud and realised that it all came back to the change of schools and the arguments at the start of the summer.

So, I just blurted it out – as I seem to do nowadays – while Mum was locking the front door.

"Sorry for the way I behaved in the summer," I began.

"What do you mean, love?" asked Mum, approaching me in the hall.

We walked into the kitchen, where Dad was pouring himself a whiskey.

"I just wanted to say that I really like my school, my teacher and my friends and none of that would have happened, if you hadn't moved me from Horley to Netherlea."

Dad put his arm around Mum (I think he'd had a few to drink – Mum had driven home) and seemed to take a breath as Mum smiled at me.

"We are thrilled at how it has all turned out too," said Mum. "We love your friends, we think your teacher is great and we're just happy that you are so settled, so soon. We don't want anything to change. Do we, love?"

Dad all of a sudden looked a bit pale.

"Love?" questioned Mum. "Are you OK?"

He sat down at the table.

"Both of you. Sit down a minute will you. There's something that I want to talk to you about."

And *THAT* was how we found out that Izzy's dad's company was expanding.

That the new contract, which Dad had been working so hard on that it had been keeping him up in the night, had been signed, which would – as Dad had predicted – mean BIG changes.

That Izzy's dad was going to have to open an office in America, in the state of North Carolina, to run the contract and that Izzy's dad (John) had approached Dad, that very night, and asked him if he was interested in running it, which was a huge deal and would mean lots more money, but would also mean that we would all have to move to the USA.

What do you say to that?

THE END

The characters in this story are completely fabricated.

During my career in teaching, I have come across several Izzys, Daisys, Jesses, Archies and, indeed, a Yusuf, an Oscar and an Carly, but while I have used their names, the personalities and characteristics were completely created by me and bear no resemblance to those children, or any of the many other wonderful students that I have had the great pleasure to teach.

Most of the other character names are 'borrowed' from colleagues, friends and family and I hope that they will see this as a compliment, as this is certainly how it was intended.

Martin Clayton
July – November 2018.

About the author:

Martin is better known as Mr C (his alter-ego), who teaches and inspires Year 6 children; encouraging them to laugh, enjoy themselves and to have the confidence to be different.

He lives in the beautiful Holme Valley with his wife, Ali, his children Paddy and Billie-Rose and the cats (Mrs Kennedy, Suzie Socks, Greyscale and Mr Biscuit).

Lightning Source UK Ltd.
Milton Keynes UK
UKHW010423150619
344455UK00001B/111/P